Inferni Ensium: Conception

Written by: Z.J. Markel

Inferni Ensium: Book 1
Conception

Z.J. Markel

Learn more about Inferni Ensium at
www.PurifiedMadness.com
or PurifiedMadness on Social Media

Sword drawn by Neomart Estudios

Copyright © 2021 Z.J. Markel

Chapter #1

It is an early summer morning, in a small settlement by the water, a modest village by the name of Stonewater. The cries of a woman in labor can be heard throughout the village, from dusk until the dawn. All through the night she pushed and strained as the father drank to dull his hearing. She lies bare upon her birthing bed, a large pad of bound straw wrapped in a simple woven blanket. The top of the bed is built like a small wooden chair, with little for a seat, to help the mother push out her child. By her side is her chosen birthing maid, an older woman by the name of Unet, a friend from the town.

The father minds his distance, giving them plenty of room to do the duty. After many hours of pain and pushing, comes a baby boy. Quite large, bless his mother, and as the boy is brought into the world, he begins to cry. Unet quickly reaches down between the mother's tired legs and lifts him in her arms, allowing the mother to caress him against her chest, "Shh, shh, shh little one. Your mother is here."

Her name is Tanta; a somewhat tall woman with long, black hair, deeply red eyes, and smooth, dark tan skin. Gentle and kind in nature, soft spoken yet strong of will. The father stands with his knife in one hand and a bottle in his other, "Finally, an end to the screams. Shall I cut the rope?"

The name of the father is Creighton Vordana; a large and rugged man, light tan of skin, and lots of little scars from years as a professional swordsman. Light brown eyes, vibrant blonde hair, and a clean-shaven face. A warrior by birth, blessed with a very imposing look, and a proud and forceful personality to boot. Dressed in all black and grey-green, except for his boots which are of dark brown leather and the details of his jacket which are of a bright yellow threading, as to match his hair. Creighton also dons a strongly made cape, that reaches down to his calves.

He approaches Tanta and his new son, kneels down, grabs the rope connecting the child to his mother. He looks to Unet for approval, who is taking care of the excess from the birth. She says "Leave some the length of your big finger." Creighton nods, and cuts it with one swift motion, leaving a bit of it still attached to the boy. Tanta barely notices, looking down at her creation with a wide smile. She looks up to Creighton and whispers "What should we name him?" Crieghton returns his knife to its sheath and places his hands on his hips, "No questions about it. His name is Creighton, Creighton Vordana the Second." Tanta looks back down at the boy "Fitting. He will be strong like his father." Creighton sits down next to her, Tanta brushes what little hair is upon the boy's head with her finger.

Creighton drapes his arm around her shoulders and looks at the boy, "That is a mighty fine boy we have made, Tanta.

He looks much like you." He does take very much after his mother; black hair, darker skin, and after a moment, they can see that his eyes share the same red of Tanta. They both stare in silence for a few moments, Unet stands up and stretches her arms, "You are not torn nor bleeding, and I have set the bag aside, to do as you please. If I may, I will be going home." Tanta looks up at her and says "You may. Thank you again, Unet." With that, the woman turns and lets herself out of the home.

After she has gone, Creighton speaks again, "I will admit to you my love, I did not think to be a father... and yet here I am." Creighton says with a tinge of worry in his voice. Tanta leans her head against him, "You will do just fine. You have fought many battles, this is but another." Creighton laughs, "Ha, war is simple. I can kill a man with little trouble, but to raise one? That is a much more complicated battle." He takes a drink from the bottle he was holding earlier, then shakes the bottle at Tanta, who looks at it with tired eyes. "Have a drink, it will help numb any pain."

Tanta grasps the bottle in one hand and takes a small sip, letting out a small cough as it hits her throat. She hands it back to Creighton, "Ugh, what was that?" she asks with a sour look. "Not sure, really. I took it from one of those fellows from across the sea." Creighton says with a chuckle, then takes a drink, "Burns like fire the first few times, but it gets better." Creighton looks at his son and reaches over to touch his head. He pulls his hand back and wipes it on his shirt, "Are they supposed to be this, viscid, when they come out?" Tanta chuckles, "Yes Creighton." Creighton reaches into his pocket and pulls out a small white cloth, he begins wiping the head of the baby.

Tanta looks back down, watching as her husband slowly cleans off their child, and thought crosses her mind. "Creighton," she said with a sad tone, he looked into her eyes. "Do you miss it?" Confused, Creighton asks "What?" "Living on the battlefield, what you were doing before. Traveling the territories, being paid to fight. Do you miss that life?"

Creighton stops cleaning off the boy, "Of course I do." Creighton takes his hand off the boy and places it on Tanta's cheek, "However that part of my life is over. I will always think of my time on the warpath with a level of fondness, but here is where I belong now." Creighton kisses Tanta on the forehead, then pats the boy on the top of his head." Tanta smiles, "I am happy to hear this."

Creighton looks over toward the window, and he can see that the sky is at its darkest. The sun will be up soon. "Well, judging by the sky, I believe it is time to go hunt." Tanta nods in agreement. Creighton begins to stand "I will go see if Joppa has awakened yet, and we will kill something." Creighton goes to walk out the front door, but Tanta speaks up. "Oh, and please go see Adlin about that doll I asked him to make." Creighton smiles and nods, "I will." He walks out of the door and shuts it behind him, he hears the child begin to whine through the window. "Perfect timing…" Creighton says under his breath.

Creighton walks down the cobbled road of his village, there is a light moisture on the ground from the previous day's rain, and some of his neighbors are beginning to wake. The village is very small, less than eighty people, located in the middle of the woodlands. It serves the lifestyle that he desires to live quite well; Away from large cities, lots of opportunity for hunting, but not completely barren. He walks down to the end of a short row of houses and pounds on the door, "Joppa! It is time to hunt." There is a short silence, and Creighton raises his fist to pound on the door once again, "Alight, you bastard. Give me a moment…"

Creighton chuckles to himself and leans against the wall of Joppa's house, folding his arms and waiting. The home is a very modest structure, like most others in the village. Constructed of simple peeled wood and thick nails, the windows are but two crossed pieces of lumber, with a set of wood and leather shutters on the inside. The floor consists of many flat stones, fitted together and held in place with simple pitch. It is a comfortable home to be sure. Joppa himself is a tall and slender man, with pale skin. Hollow of cheek but broad of shoulder, with short black hair, and small, somewhat sunken eyes.

He is known as the best bowman in the territory, if not the surrounding territories as well, and was highly praised for this during his time in King Stoen's Legion, which is where the two men met, Joppa and Creighton. *"Those were good days"* Creighton thinks to himself. They both took part in Stoen's "revolution", however the two of them were only in it for the promises of wealth and land, a point that they bonded over. Once the war was over and Samuel sat on the glorified chair, the two of them ended up settling in the same town, granted their property as a gift from their ever-so-grateful new King. As well as a fair bit of coin.

Deep in his thoughts of the old Legion, suddenly Joppa Jak jerks his door open. He has a shortbow in his left hand and a quiver strapped on his right thigh. "Took you long enough." Creighton says, leaning off the wall. "Pleasant morning to you too, Vordana." Joppa replies in a tired voice. Joppa Jak is dressed in his standard preferred attire of choice, a light tan jacket with a hand stitched undershirt, today it was bright white, almost matching his skin. Also a pair of brown pants, and tanned deer-leather short boots. One thing he never left his home without, no matter the sun or how thick the air, was his beloved short scarf. It is white, with thick red cross-stitching at each end, and a crossing pattern inked in black all across it.

"Please tell me the child was worth all the screaming." Joppa says with a smack to his own cheek, trying to bring clarity into his mind. Creighton rolls his shoulders, "A boy, about two feet long, looks healthy." Joppa smiles "Glad to hear. Now let us go, the prey are not going to kill themselves." "Agreed," Creighton said as they walk toward the woods. "His name is Creighton, the Second." Joppa smirks and glances at Creighton, now Creighton the First, "I am not surprised."

Creighton and Joppa make their way out of town and into the woods down a muddy path, Creighton walking ahead of Joppa. They are silent for a short while, keeping their eyes peeled for any kind of animal fit for eating, the only sound they hear is the wet dirt sucking at their boots. They reach the end of the muddy path and into the heart of the woods, where the prey are most likely to be. Creighton steps into the dirt, his boot sinks up to his ankle with a wet plop, "Damned rain," he says irritatedly, "it is worse here than on the path." Creighton takes a few labored steps, the wet earth consuming his foot with each step, "It is times like this when I envy the birds."

Joppa is stopped not far ahead, crouching in place and staring intently at something. Creighton makes his way to Joppa's side and crouches down. "What do you see?" Creighton whispers. "Large hare, straight ahead," Joppa said, pointing in the direction of the animal. Creighton squints, looking for the hare. "I do not see it..." he said, confused. Joppa pulls up his shortbow and notches an arrow, "Watch the arrow" Joppa says to Creighton.

He pulls back, takes a breath, and releases. The arrow flies through the air and catches the hare in the head, causing it to hop in the air upon impact and flop to the ground. "Oh, there it is." Creighton stood up, "Quite the shot Joppa." Joppa hung his bow over his shoulder with a smirk on his face, "Of course it was."

Creighton and Joppa walk up to the dead hare, which was about fifty meters away, Creighton picks it up by the rear leg, "This little bastard is a hefty one." He grabs the arrow that had pierced the skull and yanks it out with one hard pull. "Here you are my friend." Creighton says as he hands it back to Joppa. Joppa pulls out a clean cloth and wraps it around the arrow, pulling it through and cleaning it in the process. Creighton takes a piece of small rope and ties the hare to his belt by the rear legs, "Back to the hunt." Joppa nods and they make their way further into the woods.

The two of them walk in silence for a while, keeping to the roots the best they could. After a short time the sound of bubbling water is close by, "I can hear the water from here." Joppa says to Creighton. "I could use a drink," Creighton responds, walking toward the sound. Before he can step onto the stone, Joppa places his hand onto Creighton's chest, stopping him. "As could the deer," replies Joppa, pointing down-stream. Creighton looks where Joppa is pointing, about one hundred meters away is a doe and a buck, drinking from the river.

Creighton and Joppa crouch down, not wanting to spook the animals. "Which one are you aiming for?" Creighton asks quietly, "The doe, better for eating." Joppa responds. He slowly reaches into his thigh quiver and pulls an arrow, he notches it and slowly draws. "As you will, Joppa..." Creighton whispers. Joppa steadies his hands, takes a deep breath, then releases the arrow. It flies and pierces the doe straight through the heart. The doe drops with a small cry, causing the buck to jump in surprise, quickly retreating into the woods. Creighton reaches over and claps Joppa on the neck, "Wonderful work, my friend." The two of them stand and saunter over to the doe, who had quickly expired from its injury. Creighton crouches down and cuts the neck, just to be sure of its passing. He then wrests out the arrow, handing it back to Joppa.

"I can give the fur to Tanta. She may fashion you a new jacket, she has been wanting to hone her tailoring since coming with child." Joppa nods, "That would be appreciated." Creighton kneels down by the rear of the deer, Joppa walks up to the head, and the two roll it onto its back. Creighton pulls out his dressing knife and makes an incision between the legs of the doe, cutting up toward the ribs. As he is doing this, Joppa walks up to the edge of the river and sits down on the bank.

Joppa first pulls out his water bladder and holds it out under the small waterfall that runs down to feed the stream. He takes a small drink, then places it back to his belt. Joppa reaches into his quiver and pulls out two arrows, the two that had been used previously. He takes them and dips them into the stream, effectively rinsing the remaining blood from them. The current of this stream is much stronger than it appears, making for a good cleaning tool. Joppa takes a deep breath, and rolls his head, sending cracks through his neck and upper back. There were few things like an early hunt to start the day for Joppa.

While Joppa rests by the bank, Creighton has made progress with the dressing, extracting the insides, making damn sure not to puncture the bile sac or intestines. Few smells as wretched as that, Creighton knows, and given his extensive battlefield experience, he may know it all too well. Creighton begins to ponder if he should keep the head, or just cut it off and save a few pounds. Not much meat on deer face, afterall. However his thoughts are interrupted by the sound of something running up behind him.

Creighton quickly turns and attempts to stand, only to be struck by a charging wolf and knocked onto his back, Creighton's dressing knife falling from his hand. The beast attempts to bite onto Creighton's face, but he is able to put up his left arm and catch its teeth with his forearm. As the wolf bites his arm repeatedly, Creighton is trying to grasp for his dressing knife with his free hand. The wolf then moves its head and bites into Creighton's exposed hand, *"AAAGH!"* He cries out in pain.

Joppa has seen what is happening and picks up his bow, notching an arrow. While he is confident in his archery, the wolf is much too up-close to Creighton, and the two are moving too much to guarantee a hit on only the wolf. Blood is running out of Creighton's hand, dripping down into his eyes and the wolf continues to bite down and shake. Through the blood, Creighton sees that his knife is just out of reach of his fingertips, *"FORGET THE KNIFE"* he thinks to himself, as he balls his free fist and propels it into the head of the wolf, catching it in the eye.

The wolf is stunned, but does not relinquish Creighton's hand. Joppa approaches the two of them, but before he can get in and grab the wolf, Creighton screams "Back up!" Joppa is taken aback by the command, and stops in his tracks. Creighton pulls back and slams his fist into the wolf's head once more, this time striking it in the ear, and the wolf releases Creighton's hand. Creighton takes his left hand and grabs the wolf by the leg, and quickly reaches up behind the head of the wolf with his right hand, and grabs the wolf by the snout. He squeezes the leg of the wolf to hold it in place, and with all the wrathful strength in his body, yanks the head of the wolf as hard as he can around the back of itself, snapping its neck and nearly turning its head to the opposite side.

With the break, the wolf goes limp, dying near-instantly, and collapses on top of Creighton. Creighton shoves the wolf off of himself, still hyperventilating from rage and the warrior surge. Joppa walks up to him, kneels down, and places his hand on Creighton's shoulder, who looks back up at him. "Your hand is bleeding greatly", Joppa says to Creighton, who picks up his arm and looks at it. "Oh, so it is..." Creighton sits up and squeezes his left wrist, attempting to slow the leaking of blood. Joppa reaches into his satchel and pulls out a long bandage, "Give me your hand". Creighton holds his arm out to Joppa, and Joppa begins to wrap his torn up hand.

He glances over at the wolf, "Why did you not want me to grab it?" Joppa asks. Creighton takes a large breath, "It attacked me, so *I* was going to kill it." Joppa lets out a small chuckle, "Always the spiteful one." he says as he finishes the wrapping. Creighton looks at his hand, "Thank you Joppa." Joppa extends his right hand, and Creighton takes it, pulling him up to his feet. "You are welcome, my friend." The two of them look down at the dead wolf, "He seems to be starved," Joppa comments as he looks around the riverbank, "and alone by the looks of things. He must have been desperate." Creighton kicks the lifeless body, "It should have waited for the scraps, then it may still live."

The two of them both turn to the doe, Joppa grabs one of its legs, Creighton puts his hand on Joppa's shoulder. "I have this, my friend." He then crouches down, grabs a front leg and a back leg of the doe, and pulls it up onto his shoulders, grunting heavily, undoubtedly due to the pain in his hand. "Do you have a good grip on that?" Joppa asks, concerned. "Do not worry Joppa, I am hurt, not weak." Creighton grunts as he extends his legs, picking the deer up on his shoulders. Joppa nods, "As long as you have it." The two of them begin to walk back into the woods.

As they trudge through the muddy woods, their kill in hand, Joppa pulls a short-arrow from his quiver and begins to play with it in his right hand, between his middle and index finger. "We really should get together and try to make some kind of a path through these woods." Creighton says, "Just pull down a row of trees, lay some stones. It would take some time, but damn, it would be worth the trouble." Joppa nods. "That it would. However, I do not think I am going to stay in the village for much longer." Creighton looks at Joppa, "Oh really? Where are you going?"

Joppa shrugged, "My sister is up to the north, a town named Starlight. I received a message a few moons ago. She is sick, so I thought I would go and attempt to see her, before she dies. Besides, I have thought about leaving for a time now." Joppa puts his arm down and flicks the short-arrow back into his quiver. Creighton nods his head slightly, "You do what you must, my friend. Know that you will be missed." Joppa chuckles, "I am sure. Who else is going to put up with you?" Creighton smiles, "Tanta, and hopefully my son." Joppa looks at Creighton, "You will make a fine father, do not worry yourself. Now let us get this back home, I am starved."

Joppa and Creighton arrive back at their village, the sun is high and their neighbors have awakened. They approached Joppa's home, "I will butcher the kill, you have Tanta look at your hand." Joppa says to his friend. Creighton hoists the doe over his shoulders and drops it to the ground with a meaty thud. He pulls the hare off his belt and hands it to Joppa, "I shall leave you to it then".

With that Creighton turns around and starts walking back to his home. He picks up his left hand and flexes it, "Damn that hurts." he mumbles under his breath. One of his neighbors walks out of his house, "Pleasant morning, Kala." Creighton says to the man, who nods at Creighton and hurries on his way. Creighton pays it no mind as he approaches his home and grabs the handle, but pauses. He waits for a moment, *"Silence, good"* he thinks to himself.

Creighton opens the door to his home and walks in quietly. Inside, Tanta is asleep, with their new son at her breast, also resting. *"I best not disturb either of them."* Creighton thinks as he quietly walks over to their table. He takes off his, now bloody, jacket and tosses it to the floor gently. He then walks over to a cabinet and pulls out a short roll of white cloth, he places it on the table next to his bottle of mystery liquor.

Creighton sits down at the table and unwraps his hand, revealing the bloody wound across the back and palm of his hand, thankfully little damage done to the fingers. *"This is going to burn..."* he thinks as he grabs the bottle of liquor. He places his hand palm up on the table and slowly pours the drink onto the wound, to clean it. Creighton inhales sharply and squeezes the bottle tightly, trying to keep his mouth shut. He puts down the bottle and takes a deep breath.

Creighton takes some of the white cloth and dries his hand. He then rips off a piece off the roll, wads it up, and pushes it into his palm. He grimaces in pain, louder than he expected to. Tanta opens her eyes, looking around the home, she sees Creighton sitting at the table with the bandages out. "Creighton?" Tanta says, still partially asleep. Creighton shakes his head, "All is well Tanta, continue your rest." Tanta tightened her grip on the child and stood up, "Clearly not, you are bleeding. One moment." Tanta hurriedly walks over to their bed and lays the baby down, still asleep. Tanta hurries back over to the table and sits across from Creighton.

She took his hand in hers and examined it, "This is quite the wound, what happened?" Creighton rolls his neck "Wolf, trying to take our kill." Tanta nods and grabs the bandages,

"I assume the animal is worse off than you?" Creighton smiles "Of course." Tanta begins wrapping his hand tightly, "I would expect no less from my warrior." She finishes wrapping his hand and ties the bandage in place, he pulls back his hand and flexes.

"That should keep for the day, I will change it in the morning." Tanta said, caressing his hand lovingly, "Please be careful out there." Creighton puts his hand on hers, comfortingly. He looked over to their bed, "How is the boy?" Tanta stands up and walks over to the bed, "He is well. I fed him until he had his fill and we both slipped into sleep. I am just glad he seems healthy." Tanta kneels next to the bed and places her hand on the baby's head.

Creighton walks over to Tanta and places his hand on her shoulder, "I am glad the two of you are healthy. He is a large boy, is he not? Larger than I have seen before." Tanta nods, "I, he certainly felt large. I have witnessed many women give birth, and he seems a fair bit bigger than I have seen." There is a short pause as the two of them look at their sleeping child. "Joppa is leaving." Creighton says glumly, Tanta looks up at him, "Oh? Where is he going?" Creighton takes his hand off her shoulder and starts caressing his wounded hand, "He claims his sister is sick, she lives to the North. He wishes to see her before she leaves this life."

Tanta looks back down at the boy, "I wish him well. He will be missed." Creighton steps past Tanta, bends over, and very gently picks up the baby, who stirs but does not wake. "Yes, it will be quite alright." Creighton pulls the baby close to his face, and touches their heads together. "I will have a new man to accompany me on my hunts, soon enough." Tanta stands and leans her head on Creighton's shoulder, "He will have to be taught to wield a bow, or we will all go hungry."

Chapter #2

Tanta sits on the bank of the river upon a large rock in her favorite red gown, the water running through her toes, and her infant son, Creighton II, swaddled on her back. She leans her head back, brushing cheeks with the boy and allowing the sun to kiss her face. It is a truly beautiful day, complimented by a small breeze and the sound of the rushing river. "Mmmmm, it is days like this where I am glad to be here. With you and your father alike." Tanta raises her hand to touch the cheek of her son, "Especially you, my child." The boy smiles at the touch of his mother, making a quiet cooing noise.

"Tanta! Are you still here?" Creighton calls from the woods, Tanta turns her head away from her child. "Yes I am, my love!" She called out to him over her shoulder. Tanta turns back to the river, splashing water with little kicks. Creighton comes out from the woodline and looks down the riverbank, spotting his wife and child.

Creighton walks over to them, his shirt in his bandaged hand and his cape not on his person. "You have been out here all day my love, you are going to catch the redness." Tanta continues to churn the water, "I will be fine, I am quite used to the sun." Creighton walks up and crouches down by her side, "As you say. How about the boy?" Tanta reaches up and touches her son's ear, "He is cool and fed, you need not worry."

Creighton stands up straight, laying his shirt on the rock next to Tanta. "The path is coming along, slowly, but well enough. The roots of the trees run much deeper than we would like, but we are managing." Tanta looks up at him, "Do not tell me my warrior is being bested by the woods." Creighton lets out a chuckle, "Not defeated, only impeded." Creighton gives Tanta a hearty slap to the shoulder, "Go home if you begin to feel faint, I shall return to the damned trees." Creighton walks away, "I shall prepare supper by moonrise", Tanta calls to her husband. "Good" Creighton responds, before venturing back into the woods.

Creighton marches back through the woods, "*We could use more working hands for this, if only Joppa had not had to leave. His assistance would be appreciated.*" Creighton thinks to himself, "*I wonder how his journey goes. He should be nearing his destination by this time.*" It has been about two weeks since Joppa left Stonewater, which was a week after he told Creighton. As Creighton walks through the woods, he looks around, listening to the wildlife and the sounds of working men in the distance. The dirt beneath his feet is nice and dry, barely a print is made beneath his boots.

Creighton made it back to the site of work after a short walk through the woods. All able-bodied men in the village were at work, which only amounted to about thirty, cutting the trees and pulling their roots. As well as two women, however sometimes that fact was sometimes doubted. Their names are Kentra and Lum Delgoss, the two of them are built very burly and muscular, especially for women. They are the daughters of the town Peacekeeper; Hatch Delgoss, a very large man himself, the age of sixty-three but as spry and witty as the average twenty year-old. The Peacekeeper is the person in a town who is essentially in charge of keeping and promoting order and quiet in the town that he lives in, as well as taking care of any miscreants that may become a bother. As an elder, and someone who is generally regarded highly by everyone in the community, the people of Stonewater have been happy to have Hatch in the role.

Kentra is the older of the sisters, by almost two years, at the age of twenty-two. Her hair is short and dark brown, with shaggy bangs that creep just past her eyebrows, which share the same color, and are a bit thicker than you would expect for a young woman. She is almost as tall as Creighton, but he still has a few inches on her. Lum is the younger and shorter of the two, by about half a head. Her hair is a bit lighter than her sister, and Lum likes to keep it longer, tied to itself in a tail that reaches about halfway down her back. Her head is a bit more round than that of Kentra, and her nose a bit smaller. The two of them share the same set of eyes, however; large, round, and blue, the kind that romantic boys write poems about.

As Creighton returns, the Degloss daughters are working together to carry two large logs, one under each of their arms, back toward the village. "Fine work to us all! If we continue like this, we will have a clear path to the river before the white begins to fall!" Creighton calls out to all the fellow workers. "Thank you, Vordana!" calls out Hatch, "It would go faster if you actually helped!" A small chuckle spreads through the workers, Creighton ignores the jest and walks over to two men working a large saw against the base of the tree.

One of them was a well built man, the other is a slender boy, only a short time into manhood, and clearly having trouble with the saw. Creighton walks over and places his hand on the boy's shoulder, "Step aside Gesa." The boy looks up at Creighton, then steps out of his way without a word. Gesa Het, a young man of eighteen years, not weighing more than 150 pounds or standing taller than 5'8". Very pale skinned, and sandy brown hair. Creighton grabs the side of the saw, he and the other man begin to quickly push and pull the tool back and forth, quickly working their way through the trunk.

As they near the backside of the trunk, the tree begins to fall with the angle of the cut. "Tree down!" Creighton calls out, as the tree falls with a deep and loud *thud!* Before the branches have time to settle, two men and one of the Delgoss daughters run over, beginning to branch and quarter it to be moved. Creighton wipes the sweat from his forehead with the back of his arm, "One cut, only an uncounted number to go..." The boy, Gesa, walks over to Creighton with a wooden cup filled with water in his hand, "For you sir." Creighton snatches the cup from his hand, causing Gesa to flinch back, "Much appreciated, boy." Creighton swallows the full contents of the cup in one go, then tosses it back into the hands of Gesa.

"Now then..." Creighton looks around, "You three!" Creighton points to a group of three men putting their axes to tree roots. "Go down to the river and begin to gather stones for the path!" The three men look at Creighton, then one another, then drop their tools and begin walking toward the river, "Yes Vordana." replies one of the men out loud. "They should be smooth and ideally as flat as possible! We want to manually smooth as few as we can." Creighton calls at them. One of the men grumbles beneath his breath, not speaking out loud. "Why must we gather the damn rocks?" one man asked quietly, "Because he told us to, and I will not be the one to question him" Another replies, looking over his shoulder. "Aside, I do not mind taking on a task where I am not around him." They all look back toward Creighton, who has begun to help cut the roots of another tree, then turn back toward their destination. "The smug bastard..."

His ax in hand, Creighton swings it high above his head, bringing it down on a particularly thick root. As the wood is cleaved away, Creighton cannot help but have a small grin. He enjoys this kind of physical, taxing labor. It helps him feel strong, as he felt in his days as a mercenary, out on the warpath. The deep ache in his hands and joints remind Creighton of the feeling of battle, striking down an opposing man. A feeling that has faded from him in the recent years, it almost made him long for the conflict.

Creighton finally works his ax through the root, cleaving through the last bit of wood and getting stuck in the dirt. He pulls the ax free and places it over his shoulder, Creighton scratches the back of his head with his other hand, and takes a deep breath. "Vordana, sir" a voice speaks from behind Creighton, he turns around to face the voice, it is Gesa. "What do you want?" Gesa looks at the ground nervously, "How do you, do that?" Creighton is confused by the question, "Do what?" Gesa looks up at him, "Well, everything. Saw trees, chop wood, carry a dead deer by yourself." Gesa starts rubbing his right arm, "I cannot do any of that."

Creighton hands his ax to Gesa, "Take this." Gesa takes the ax in both hands, as Creighton releases his grip, Gesa's arms sag slightly at the weight of the tool. "You are weak, gawky even. That is your problem." Gesa looks up at Creighton, "How do I get stronger, sir?" Creighton grabs the ax from

Gesa's hands and starts working on another tree root. "Ask your father, boy." As Creighton begins working, Lum comes over and begins cutting at a different root on the same stump.

Gesa is directly behind Creighton, "I have-" Gesa has to quickly duck to avoid the backswing of Creighton's ax. Gesa steps safely to the side, "But he has not given me much advice." Creighton continues to chop away, "It is a lot of work. Work hard, eat well, and sleep. You can not grow muscle well on an empty belly or an exhausted body." "I have been working, you saw me helping to cut that tree. It does seem to affect me." Gesa says with a whine in his voice.

Creighton rolls his eyes a little and opens his mouth, however Lum Delgoss speaks up before he can get a word out. "It, does not, happen quickly, Gesa." she says between swings of her ax. Lum lifts the ax straight over her head and brings it down into the root, busting through the root and sticking in to the dirt, then letting go. Lum faces Gesa and Creighton and flexes her arms, "Despite what many may think about myself and my family, none of us were born with these muscles." Lum punches her right fist into her opposing palm with a *Thump*, "We had to do much physical labor, for many months and years before our muscles begin to bulge."

Lum grabs her ax and yanks it from the ground with minimal effort, "It takes much time and discipline, and if you start to feel like you are about to fall apart, that means it is working." Lum takes her ax in both hands, "That aside, if you cannot grow your body, I would not worry so much." Lum lifts up her ax and brings it down with great force, cutting a medium-sized root in one strike, separating it from the rest. Lum looks at Gesa with a smirk, "Some women like smaller men."

Creighton had continued to chop during this conversation, "She is right, mostly. All it takes is time, effort, and dedication. With those three things, you can become as large as her father." Lum looks at Creighton, "Let us not get his hopes high." Gesa nods, "Thank you both." Creighton stops chopping and stands up straight, "In fact..." Creighton thrusts the ax into Gesa's arms, he stumbles back a step while clutching the tool to his chest, "You can start now."

Creighton begins to walk away, he looks back at Lum, "Make sure the boy does not kill himself, or anyone else." Lum smiles and crouches down, grabbing at the tree stump that they have just cut free, "I do not think he could if he wanted to." Lum then stands, gripping the bottom of the tree stump, and pulling it the rest of the way free from the dirt. As she flips it over, she claps Gesa on the back, almost knocking the boy off his feet.

Creighton walks over to the water barrel and grabs himself a cup to drink from. "Creighton, my Love!" Tanta's voice calls out from a short distance away, Creighton looks toward her. "What is it?" Tanta stands on the edge of the work site, Creighton II still on her back, in her hand she holds a parchment; a green parchment. Creighton knows what that means immediately; a message from King Stoen himself. He tosses the cup back into the barrel and jogs up to Tanta, he takes the parchment from her hand and hurries her along. "Come, come. This must be read in private."

Chapter #3

Creighton nudges Tanta into the door of their home, he closes and locks the door behind them with a wooden latch. "Where was this?" Creighton asked in a deadly serious tone, "It was placed on the bottom of the window, held by a small rock. It was there when I returned home." Tanta says as she pulls her son off her back, cradling him in her arms. "Do you think it is urgent?" Tanta sits at the table, Creighton stares at the parchment, "He does not send messages to ask how we fare. If he took the time to write and have it delivered this far, it must be of some importance."

Samuel Stoen is the reigning King of the Lockhart territory, where Creighton and Tanta live. Lockhart is the capital city for which the territory is named, and home of the king. Creighton served Stoen loyally during his rebellion against the now late King, Alestin Drow. Once the movement had come to the conclusion, and the blood had dried, Creighton, along with all other generals, were given the option to either retire with their reward, or continue to serve the Stoen regime. Creighton, Joppa, and a few others chose to take their due and be on their way, which Stoen respected.

Creighton sits across from Tanta and opens the parchment. Creighton II begins to whine, Tanta bounces him in her arms gently, "Shh, shh, shh my son. Is your belly empty?" Tanta takes a moment and begins feeding her son, then she looks up to Creighton, "Well, what does it say?" Creighton does not respond for a moment, "King Stoen says that over the last few seasons, he has received reports about his old generals being killed. Two have died this last season alone." Tanta puts her hand to her mouth, "How terrible. Any friends of yours?"

Creighton shakes his head, "Deka Jumall, Adrick Serint, names I recognize but do not deeply care for. That is not the disturbing part, however, the part that breeds worry is this." Creighton places the paper face up on the table, Tanta looks at it. The message was written in white ink to stand out from the dark green of the paper itself. "All of the generals who have been killed were either alone, if they were in the woods or in another form of seclusion. Or in their homes, and any who were nearby slaughtered alongside. Mauled by what seem to be wolves."

Tanta shakes her head, "Then how is he sure they are all murders?" Creighton shrugs and stands from his chair, "Unless there is a sword wielding wolf leading its pack around the territories, it is doubtful." Creighton leans on the wall by their cooking fire. "While the people of the towns are ripped and torn apart, the generals are killed the same way every time. Clean beheading." Tanta clutches her son to her chest a little harder, "So, does that mean..." Creighton looked back at his wife, "It means that somebody is killing old King Stoen generals from the Legion, and they do not want anyone to know who they are."

Creighton walks over to Tanta, "He says to be wary of strangers, especially any who bring dogs." He kneels down in front of his wife and child, "Rest assured, that I will not let any man, woman or hound harm you or my child. Do you understand?" Tanta nods her head, "I understand and believe you my love. We should tell the rest of the town." Creighton stands and snatches the paper off the table. "No, we should not." Creighton gives the paper one last look-over, then casts it into the fire. "Stoen said not to spread word of this. He fears that if people hear that villages of people are being slaughtered right under his watch, especially with a pattern as clear as this, people would begin to panic, and to doubt him."

Tanta stands, "To the Fire Lands with his pride. We may be attacked!" Creighton turns around quickly, "If we are, I will protect you and the boy, and if we are not, all we will have done is stir up the townsfolk and sow doubt of their ruler in their hearts." "What about our companions?" Tanta asked, "If trouble comes, they should be prepared anyway. As they have before." Tanta steps back and sits on the edge of their bed, "Should we leave?" Creighton crosses his arms, "No. This is our home, and I will not be scared into hiding." Tanta looks up, "But-" Creighton puts out his hand, "Do not continue to speak." Tanta hangs her head, looking down at her infant son, who has finished feeding. Tanta pulls him up and clutches him to her shoulder.

Creighton takes a deep breath, "There have been eight known generals killed in the last few years. Those last two lived in the same part of the territory. There were over forty generals in King Stoen's Legion. The odds of them finding me and coming here are low." Creighton takes Tanta's chin in his hand, making her look at him, "If he ever does, then I will cut him down, and his companions, and his dogs, and anyone else who assists him. You need not be troubled." Creighton caresses her cheek, "Now I will have no more talk of this. You are safe for as long as I draw breath." Tanta smiles and touches his hand, "I know that my love, I am sorry if I implied otherwise."

Creighton leans in and kisses Tanta on her lips, and gives his son a pat on his head, whose hair has grown out quite a bit. "Hm, black hair, like his mother." Creighton says under his breath as he stands up straight. "Now, I will be getting back to those trees. Thank you for bringing that message to my attention, my love." Creighton walks toward the door. "Be cautious out there." Tanta says as he walks out of their home. She glances into the fire, the green parchment is almost gone, what is left is curled and black, small embers flicking off of it.

Creighton slowly walks back toward the path site, *"Maybe we should tell people. Allow them to prepare, if this event ever comes to pass."* Creighton thinks to himself. Two men carrying a large log walk pass by, Creighton pays them no mind, *"However they should be prepared for an attack no matter what. Raiders, worshippers... or wolves. It is not my responsibility to make sure these people are fit to defend their own lives."* Deep in his thoughts, Creighton bumps into Kentra Delgoss, causing her to drop her ax and bag upon impact, however she herself stays upright.

"I did not know you were blind, Creighton." Kentra shoves Creighton back, stumbling him a step. "I apologize for the bump, but do not shove me, girl." Kentra puts her fist on her side, "You think I am scared of you, like the others?" Creighton begins to walk around Kentra, "No, you are not that smart." Creighton takes a few steps past, but suddenly is stopped by a grip on his belt. "Let go of my belt, girl." Creighton says without turning around. "Ramming into me is one thing, but you are insulting me to my face, and that, I can not let go." Creighton turns around and Kentra goes chest to chest with him, although despite her large build, is still shorter than him.

"I want you to apologize." Kentra says with a straight face. Creighton takes a deep breath, "Take, a step, back." Kentra crosses her arms over her chest, not saying a word. Creighton glares into her eyes, trying to decide if this fight is worth having. "Ey, ey, ey, stop it now." Hatch Delgoss comes jogging over to the two of them. Creighton and Kentra's altercation has caught the attention of everyone working, they are all watching. Hatch grabs his daughter by the shoulder and pulls her backwards, digging his fingers in, "That is enough, my daughter. You have proven your boldness, now come with me." Kentra does not break eye contact with Creighton, "No, I want him to-" Hatch quickly wraps his arm around the back of her neck and pulls Kentra's head under his arm, pressing her face into his side, "You want *nothing!*"

Hatch starts dragging Kentra back towards their home, whispering panicked words to her, loud enough for her, but too quiet for anyone else to interpret. Creighton rolls his neck, exhaling through his nostrils, and untensing his shoulders. The rest of the people return to their work, Creighton walks over to where Gesa is standing, "Gesa." The boy looks up at Creighton, who looks down at where Gesa was cutting, he has barely made a dent in what he was working on. Creighton grabs the ax from Gesa's hands, almost pulling the boy off his feet, "Go."

Gesa runs away, wordless, Lum looks at Creighton, "What was that with Kentra?" Creighton grips the ax firmly, "Your older sibling does not know what wars should be instigated, it seems." Lums tosses her ax lightly in her hands. "That sounds appropriate for her." Creighton raises his ax above his head and brings it down viciously, hacking away at the dead tree as though it were an abhorred foe. Lum gives

Creighton a moderately concerned glance, but puts her head down and returns to chopping.

-

Night has fallen on the town of Stonewater, Creighton Vordana sits silently by the fire of his home, dressed in his day attire with his cape around his shoulders. In his right hand lay his prime sword, the one he has carried on his hip since the beginning of his manhood. His mother had stitched his sheath from tat bull hide, to accompany the sword. In his left hand he holds a whetstone.

Creighton takes the stone and gingerly places it to the edge of the blade, sliding it down the length of the steel with a dull hiss. Creighton looks over to his bed, in it is his wife, cuddling their infant child tightly. Creighton continues to slowly smooth the blade of his sword, staring at his family, and thinking. Many thoughts danced within his mind; the message from King Stoen, the travels of his friend Joppa, his future as a father... and the disrespect of the Delgoss girl. Despite everything, that is what pricks him the most. Like a small thorn in his neck, a burr in his boot. That little act of contempt, it bothered him deeper than even he understood why. Creighton takes the stone and sets them on the table to his side.

He finds himself wishing that Joppa had not left. He had been primary confidant for Creighton since their time in Stoen's Legion, Joppa had always had some piece of wisdom for any occasion. However, Creighton knows that he cannot mope about Joppa's leaving, like a young boy losing a pet. It was just a shame. Creighton knows that he could speak with Tanta about anything in confidence, but there are certain things that men keep from their wives. A husband is supposed to be strong, confident. He does not wish to imply that he is anything else to Tanta, no matter how minor, or how valid.

He stands and slides his sword into its sheath. Creighton walks out of his home quietly, not wanting to wake Tanta or the boy, and gently closing the door behind him. The air is cold and crisp, he can taste the moisture. Creighton walks toward the newly torn path, it is almost half completed, another week or so of work and it will be ready to lay stone. Creighton begins to walk down the path, the only sounds are of the light breeze and the insects buzzing or chirping. Creighton reaches the end of the torn path and begins on the dirt, walking towards the river.

The earth is moist from the mist, yet still solid underfoot. After a short while, Creighton reaches the rocky edge of the river. Creighton walks over to a large rock, the same one Tanta was sitting on earlier, and sits down cross-legged. The night has always been a peaceful time for Creighton, the time where the least conflict takes place, be it on the battlefield or otherwise.

The night was the time for peace, quiet, fellowship. Creighton places his hands on his knees and takes a deep breath in through his nostrils, taking in the crisp, moist air from the river. The sound of the rushing water was quite relaxing, such a powerful sound, but gentle and pleasant to the ear.

After some time, maybe more than ten minutes, the sound of the river is interrupted by the sound of howling. Wolves. It sends a worried chill down Creighton's spine, while wolves in the area are not uncommon, the sound becomes much more worrisome given the letter from Stoen... *"I should return home"* Creighton thinks, standing up, and turning back toward the village. *"I will not let that message drive me to madness..."* Creighton walks into the woods, and returns home for the night.

Chapter #4

The winter has passed, and spring has graced the town of Stonewater. It had been a mild winter, but still damn cold. The townsfolk had managed to finish the river path right as the first snow of the winter had begun to fall, much to both the relief and satisfaction of everyone. It has made gathering water and hunting much easier, as was the intended purpose. Creighton feels quite proud of himself for this little project that he headed up, even some of the people in town who do not care for him had to admit that it was a wise plan.

Now that the sun is shining, and the snow has all cleared away, Creighton is out behind his home, shirtless, practicing his swordsmanship on the wooden training doll that he has staked into the ground. Of course, he is not using his real sword, Creighton has several dulled blades that he uses to beat on dolls or training partners. They were all trophies from his days on the warpath for Stoen. Sometimes, when Creighton would strike someone down, if they had a sword that he fancied, he would take it and add it to his little collection of training tools. This is not something of a common practice in Oblitus, just something that Creighton thought to start doing.

The sword he is currently using is a normal longsword, with an upward-curved crossguard and a black leather wrap for the hilt. By the feel of it, it seems to be deer hide, which is usable, but not the material Creighton would have chosen. The edges of it have begun to fray slightly over the years, and the blunted blade is a bit dented from use. This sword was best relegated to a training tool. After all, it was not quality enough to save its previous owner.

He is practicing some basic combat drills, as well as some little tricks that he's learned through his career as a swordsman. Gripping the sword with both hands, then his right hand, then his left hand, switching grip between drills. One of the first things that his old teacher taught him was that sometimes you may not be able to wield your weapon the way you want. Your strong hand may be wounded or occupied, so it is important to be able to effectively use your weapon with both hands, together and independently.

As Creighton switches the sword from his right hand into his left, when he hears footsteps from behind him. "Yes?" he asks, without turning to see who it is. "Hello sir. I was wondering, if I could talk to you about some things." It was Gesa Het, half a season older than before but not a pound heavier. Creighton considers for a moment, and decides to humor the boy. He rests the blunted sword on his shoulder and turns around to face Gesa, "Go ahead. What is on your mind?"

"Well, I just saw you practicing with your sword. I was wondering if you would be so gracious as to show me how to handle a blade for myself." Gesa asks, somewhat timidly. He seems like he wants to learn, but is intimidated by the prospect. "Why do you want to learn?" Creighton asks. Gesa seems to be unprepared for this question, but after a moment he responds "Well, every man should be able to wield a blade, I feel."

With that, Creighton nods approvingly, "That is a good answer, boy. Go inside and ask Tanta for another one of my blunted blades, as well as my prime sword. Then I will show you some things." Gesa smiles and nods, immediately turning and jogging toward the front of the house. Creighton begins to mull over in his head, if he should give the boy some genuine teachings, or just smack him around a bit for the fun of it...

Inside her home, Tanta is preparing a goose that they had gotten from a wagon merchant who had come through town that morning, it was quite fresh. It reminded Tanta of her time cooking for King Drow. He had always been a fan of goose, so she had been taught how to cook it in the most delicious ways known to the territory, and now she was excited to make it for her own husband and son. As Tanta begins to pluck the goose, the front door opens up, and in comes Gesa.

"Hello, madam Vordana." the young man says, "Creighton told me to come in here and ask you about swords." Tanta is confused by this statement, as she knows very little about swords, or sword fighting, or really anything regarding swords, really. But, if Creighton told him to ask her, then she supposed that there was a reason for it. "Hmm... well what would you like to know?" she asks. Gesa looks around the inside of the home and says "Um... where they are?" *"OH! That makes more sense..."* Tanta thinks to herself.

"Yes, Gesa! What do you need?" She starts walking toward the cupboard where Creighton keeps all of his weapons and tools. "He said to ask you for one blunted, and his prime sword." Tanta opens up the cupboard, inside are several weapons hung up with care. An old bow, a few knives, one hand-hammer, and in the middle of it all is Creighton's prime sword. His blade that he carried through his whole time in Stoen's Legion; the blade is long and slim, still had its shine, with a smooth upwardly angled crossguard, dark green leather wrapped around the grip that was just long enough to be held in both hands, and a cubed pommel, which also is as shined as the blade.

Tanta pulls that one out and leans it on the wall, next to the cupboard, then crouches down and opens the wide drawer that is at the bottom of the fixture. Inside were eight swords, all of different sizes, shapes, and cuts, all deliberately blunted. Tanta looks up at Gesa, then back to the drawer, and pulls out a relatively small sword, likely a sidesword for a charge soldier. It has a blue cloth wrap around the grip, and a rounded tip, that was actually round before Creighton took the file to it. It makes Tanta think that this is a sword from someone outside of the Lockhart territory, as such a thing is not common around these parts.

Tanta stands up with the rounded sword in hand, and closes up the cupboard. She then grabs Creighton's prime sword and walks them both over to Gesa, "You be extremely careful with this one" she says, as she hands him the prime sword. "Not just because it is sharp, but if Creighton sees you drag or drop it, he very well may give you a thumping." She warns Gesa with a smirk. However, he takes this warning seriously, and thanks Tanta, before turning and leaving the doorway.

Tanta turns back to the inside, where young Creighton is dragging himself across the floor, trying to follow Gesa. Tanta crouches down and scoops the boy up into her arms, "Now, now, we can go out later. Right now, mother needs to finish what she was doing." He just looks up at Tanta and smiles. Creighton II is quite large for his age, a fair couple of stones heavier than a boy his age would normally be. However, Tanta thought little of it. "At this rate, he will make a formidable soldier" Creighton had commented just the other day, and Tanta agreed, even though the idea of her son living a life on the battlefield was a bit nerve-striking.

Outside, Gesa comes around the back of the house with the swords that Creighton demanded, and being ever so cautious with his prime sword. "Excellent" Creighton proclaims when he sees Gesa coming, "Give me my prime." Creighton sets the blunted practice sword he was using on the ground, and Gesa hands Creighton his sword. Creighton takes the grip in his right hand, and gently lays the blade in his left palm, "This, boy, is a proper sword. The one I carried ever since I graduated from being a spear-bearing charge soldier, all the way through my time in Stoen's Legion. It has seen many battles, and many foes. It is a strong and forceful weapon. I want you to touch the edge, but carefully."

 Creighton holds the sword out at arms length, Gesa looks down at it, then up at Creighton. "Go on, touch the edge with your finger." Gesa timidly reaches out and touches the edge of the sword with the pad of his thumb, "That is, very sharp" he says, pulling his hand back. "Yes, very indeed. Now, imagine that, but against your neck. Or into your head, or your chest. It would not be pleasant, would it?" Gesa shakes his head, "Exactly. I tell you this, because sword play is not a game. A real weapon fight is a lot of pain, and a lot of risk, and a real sword is not something to be brandished lightly or in jest. I wanted to establish this before I taught you anything. Now, with all that said, would you still like me to teach you?"

 Gesa looks down at the sword, then back to Creighton, and nods his head. With that, Creighton shoulders his sword and smiles "Excellent. Now, take that little toy you have there, and grip it in both hands." Creighton turns around and walks over to a wooden bench up against the back of his house, he lays his prime sword down, and walks back to where he left the boy. He picks up the blunted sword he was using before and looks at Gesa, then lets out a small laugh. Gesa has his hands wrapped around each other, gripping the hilt very tightly.

"You are not trying to strangle the sword, Gesa. Move your hands, like this..." Creighton then places his hands on the grip of his sword slowly, as to allow Gesa to clearly see. Crieghton places his right hand at the top, near the crossguard but not pressed against it, and the left hand about the width of his thumb down below, establishing a firm but flexible grip of his hilt. His arms are bent slightly and loose, the pommel of the sword pointing at Creighton's abdomen. Gesa looks down at his hands and does his best to emulate the grip that Creighton showed. Right hand up by crossguard, left hand a little under, both gripping firmly but not squeezing the handle.

Creighton looks at the boy's grip and nods, "Good enough. Now, different swords do require different grips. Such as my prime sword, it is intended to be held in two hands, and there are smaller swords that can be wielded with one hand, in tandem with a shield, or another weapon. However, this is a good place to begin. First thing after your grip, is your stance." Gesa looks down at his feet, he is flat-footed and his heels are almost touching. "With a stance like that, you are easily stumbled," says Creighton. As Gesa looks up from his feet, he is suddenly met with Creighton's palm smacking into his chest, knocking Gesa flat on his back and causing him to drop his sword. "Like that" Creighton says with a straight face, "Get back up, grip your sword, and stand like this," he then re-grips his sword, and spreads his legs shoulder-width apart, keeping his knees slightly bent, and turns his body so he is not standing flush with Gesa.

Gesa quickly grabs the blunted sword and stands back up, looking at Creighton's legs and doing his best to imitate. Creighton walks up to Gesa and thumps him in the chest again with his palm, Gesa grunts with the impact and sways back a bit, but does not fall, "Feels better already, does it not?" Gesa smiles a little and nods. Creighton steps back, "Raise your sword up, like this." Creighton shows a high guard, which Gesa quickly emulates. "Keep your grip firm. This is a standard overhead strike." With that Creighton steps in, raises his sword up, and brings it down into Gesa's blade. While Creighton did pull his swing, the impact is still enough to bounce Gesa's sword down and smack into his forehead. "Ah!" Gesa exclaims, in a combination of pain and surprise.

Creighton pays it little mind, "That is why I said to keep your grip firm. Now..." Creighton steps back and raises his sword in a high guard. "You try it." Gesa looks up at Creighton, then down at his hands around his sword. He takes a deep breath, then pulls the sword up over his shoulder and brings it down into Creighton's guard like he was swinging an ax at a log. The two swords clash with a loud *clang*, Creighton's sword barely flinches, and Gesa pulls back his sword to his chest, "How, how was that?" Creighton lowers his guard and rests his sword on his shoulder, "Absolutely terrible." Gesa hangs his head, "However, that is to be expected. The first time I used a sword, I was like a child swinging a stick. You will improve. For now, those are some of the basics. If you wish to learn to use a sword properly, you will first begin with practicing and perfecting those things."

Gesa nods his head, "Thank you, sir." Creighton glances past Gesa, then looks back at the boy and raises his sword in a ready stance, "You are welcome. However, there is one last thing that I would like to teach you. Ready your stance." Gesa quickly gets into the stance that he was just taught, "One of the most important lessons, Gesa, are you paying attention?" Gesa looks at Creighton and nods vigorously, "Yes sir, full attention." "Good. So this lesson is simple, yet vital if you are going to be a swordsman, this is something that many men on the field fail at. Now, you must always be aware of your surroundings, and never fully drop your guard. You never know when a foe may be right behind you."

As soon as Creighton says that, Gesa is suddenly tackled to

the ground from behind, by Lum Degloss, her arms wrapped around his waist. "Like me!" she shouts with a jovial tone. Creighton smiles, and steps back, resting the practice sword on his shoulder and giving Lum room to stretch Gesa. Gesa and Lum begin squealing and wrestling on the ground, Lum treating him like an older brother treats his younger. Creighton just watches and shakes his head, *"There are men who would pay for this sort of treatment, Gesa"* he thinks to himself.

Lum grabs Gesa in a headlock, trapping his arm up behind his back as well, and looks over at Creighton, "Oh Creighton, I have meant to ask, are you and Kentra still upset with one another?" Gesa is attempting to pull himself free from the burly girl, and failing. Creighton rolls his eyes, walks over, and lays the blunted sword he was holding on the ground behind the house, "The malice is more one-sided than she would like to think. I do not know why she wishes to quarrel with me." Lum now has Gesa upside down, gripping him around his stomach, his rear up next to her head, "She has this fantasy of being 'the strongest woman in the entire Lockhart Territory' or something, and you are considered the strongest man in town, so I guess she wants to use you to prove something." Creighton rolls his neck, "And yet she lacks the fortitude to actually throw a punch or make the direct challenge? How pitiful."

Lum drops Gesa down onto his front, then puts her hands

on her hips and shrugs, "I sometimes fail to understand my sister as well. Maybe she does not want an actual fight, maybe she just wants to see if she can make you be the one to back down." Gesa pushes himself up onto all fours, and Lum quickly jumps onto him, wrapping her arms around his chest and flattening him to the ground, "Well" Creighton says as he grabs his prime sword off the bench, "Gesa, once you are done beating on Lum, take that blunted sword home with you. Practice what I showed you today." Creighton begins walking toward the front of the house, "Yes, sir" Gesa says from underneath Lum, with great strain.

 Creighton walks around the front of his home, and into the front door. Right by the doorway is young Creighton II, whom Creighton crouches down and picks up with his free hand, "Hello, young man." "He has been trying to get out of the house all day." Tanta says, looking at her two men, Creighton gives a huff of a laugh, "Maybe he is trying to get out there to get to work. Finally begin to earn his meals." Tanta comes over and gives Creighton a kiss on the cheek, then Creighton II a kiss on the head, "Why did you have Gesa come in and ask about swords?" Creighton walks toward his weapon cupboard, "The boy asked me to show him a few things about sword fighting. He... well let us say he is not fit for military work. However, I have seen worse." Tanta giggles.

Chapter #5

The sun is high in the sky as well as the birds. It is a warm summer's day in Stonewater, and Creighton is down at the town butcher shop with his son sitting on his shoulder. A man named Keval and his wife are in the process of parsing apart a cow that had just been slaughtered this morning. It is a nice brick building, the walls are lined by shelves and racks covered in various meats, fish, and spices. The shop itself is fairly dark and stuffy, the air lacks any movement, as they have to keep the place closed up tight to keep the bugs and birds from coming in and helping themselves to the inventory.

Creighton II is with his father because Tanta asked for some time alone, likely to nap. Creighton does not mind though, it gives him the chance to bond with his boy a bit. At the moment, they are waiting for that fresh cow to be divided up, as Creighton's stomach is very much in the mood for some fresh meat. As they wait, Creighton and his son are looking around the shop, the father is looking at the various spices for sale, and the son is reaching out to poke at every piece of edible flesh in the building.

One spice that particularly has Creighton's interest is a little glass jar full of red flakes; the words "Fire Spice" are painted on the outside of the jar. He looks at Keval and asks "What is fire spice?" He looks up at the jar in Creighton's hand, "That is dried out and crushed up little berries, we have been getting them from our neighbors to the east. Put it on your meat and it will set your tongue ablaze! Metaphorically. But it is delicious in my opinion. I enjoy it with goose, especially, or duck." *"Set your tongue ablaze?"* Creighton thinks, before setting the jar back on the shelf.

The front door to the shop opens up and in walks the town Peacekeeper, Hatch Delgoss, proclaiming his entrance with "Ey! How are my favorite bladesmen today?!" Keval and his wife both look at him and say "We are well" at the same time. Creighton turns to face him, "Good day, Hatch." Creighton II almost falls off his shoulder while trying to poke at a strung up fish, but Creighton reaches up and catches him, straightening his back. "Ah! The two Creighton's. How are you?" "We are doing well. Just waiting for them to finish parsing that cow."

"Ah! Another thing we have in common, it seems." Hatch says and he looks over toward Keval, "How much longer on that meat, there?!" Keval shrugs, "Another hour or so." Hatch throws up his hands, "Too long! People are hungry out here!" He looks back at Creighton, "Say, while we wait, how about you come back to my home for a drink, eh?" Creighton pats his son's legs, "I would welcome it, however the boy must come too." Hatch waves Creighton to follow him as he walks toward the door, "I have no issues with that. Come now!"

The three of them walk down the street and over to Hatch's home. It is a fair-sized abode, more than enough room to comfortably fit the four of them. Hatch, his wife Unet, and his daughters Lum and Kentra. It is a wide and open house, the only two enclosed rooms being a toilet room and the sleeping quarters. In the main room is a dining table fit to seat a dozen people, and sitting at it is Unet, repairing what appears to be a shirt that had a large tear in it. "Ah, hello Creighton, and Creighton the second!" Creighton sets Creighton II down on the floor, who takes a few steps and then falls onto all fours. He is getting the hang of walking, but is not quite there.

"Is the baby here?" calls a voice from the other room, followed by Lum walking out shirtless, "Aww, there he is! Such a large child." she says as she sees Creighton II. *That is certainly a unique chest*" Creighton thinks to himself, "Lum! Do not act like a savage, we have guests." Lum waves at her father dismissively, "Oh everyone has seen a woman's chest before. How do you think he made this big creature on the floor here?" Hatch rolls his eyes and Unet then hands Lum the shirt she had been repairing, and Lum pulls it on over her head before picking up Creighton II.

Hatch looks at Creighton and gestures at the table, "Please, sit. I will grab the drink." Creighton sits down at the long table. On each side are not chairs but two large benches made from whole logs that had been shaved flat and banded with iron bands. Lum is tossing Creighton II in the air and catching him on his way down, the boy is giggling the whole time. "Oof, what do you feed this child, steak? He is so bi~ig!" Creighton nods, "Yes, as everyone has informed me these many months." It is true, as almost every single person he speaks to when the boy is around, the first thing they say is a comment on the size of the boy. *"It is not like Tanta birthed a grown man"* he thinks to himself. That notwithstanding, Creighton is also impressed at the size of the boy. It is just not something he feels needs reiterating a dozen times a day.

"Here we are!" Hatch walks back to the table with two glasses and a large purple bottle, he sets one glass in front of Creighton and fills it almost to the top, he then sits down across from Creighton, sets down his glass, and sets the bottle down. "Where is my glass?" Lum asks, "You are taking care of the child! You can have one later." he says as he takes a sip of his own drink. "Mmmmm, as tasty as it is painful."

Creighton picks up his glass, sips it, and smacks his lips, "I have had drinks with more sting." Hatch nods "As have I, but it's not a competition, ha." Creighton looks into his cup, "What exactly is this?" Hatch shrugs, "I think it is made from rice" and takes another sip. "I just know that it warms my insides." Creighton takes another sip, Hatch sets down his glass and leans on the edge of the table. "So, I heard that

Gesa boy came to you asking for swording lessons?" "Yes. He saw me practicing and asked if I could show him some things. Why?" Hatch nods, "That is good to hear, that boy could use a strong man teaching him some things."

Creighton swirls his glass in hand, "What about his father?" "Ha!" Hatch bursts out, "Have you ever met the man?" Creighton shakes his head, "I have seen him, but never spoken or made formal acquaintance." Hatch rolls his eyes and takes another sip of his drink, "I have seen more gall from poets, and the mother is not better. I am almost surprised he came to speak with you at all." Creighton had not known about that. "Why did he not come to you? Given he and your daughter's infatuation."

Hatch shrugs, "I never served, Creighton, you know that. And all young men look up to the military folk, do they not? I think that in his eyes, you are the 'perfect man'. So who better to teach him the manly arts, eh?" Creighton nods, pondering. "Besides, I think because of that infatuation, the boy might be a tad bit scared of me! Ha!"

As he takes another sip, Creighton thinks of something that he should likely speak with Hatch about. "Hatch. As the town Peacekeeper, you have an inkling of everyone's preparedness, correct?" "Prepared how?" Hatch replies. "In terms of defense. If something were to show up in the night, you would have an idea of how well equipped and such everyone would be, yes?" Hatch takes a sip from his glass,

"Aye, for the most part. Why?" "This conversation had just sparked my mind, is all. Wondering how well equipped the town would be in case of some kind of madness."

Hatch sets his cup down and strokes his stubbly chin, "Well, I would say most of the men in the town have some kind of weaponry. A sword or a wood splitting ax at the least. Most do not have any sort of armor, including yourself, correct?" Creighton nods, unhappy about that fact. "Ha, well it goes to show ya, know what challenges to take. Anyhow, I would say about… less than half of the people around here would be ready and willing if say a band of raiders decided to pay us a visit. But between yourself and my family, I bet we could take on any army!" Hatch toasts himself with his glass, spilling a little, before taking another swig.

Creighton smiles, *"Less than half…"* he thinks to himself, a discouraging sentiment for sure. However, there have been worse armies that have done fairly well for themselves...

Chapter #6

[Stoen's Legion]

Creighton is riding on the back of a wagon, surrounded by a dozen other men. He is donned in long-sleeved leather armor with brass studs all over the forearms, shoulders, and chest. His pants are thick and black, with studded leather up the sides of his thighs and all across his shins. He has a leather helmet, but is not wearing it currently, only when he is in combat. Creighton is on his way to a camp in the valley of a mountain range, the camp of the rebel Samuel Stoen. Ever since his banishment from King Drow's military, he has been amassing an army of rebels and mercenaries.

Creighton is also former military, but not in the Lockhart territory, and he has spent the last few years as a mercenary and paid enforcer. This made him greatly desired by Stoen's little rebel army, so much so that a personal recruiter was sent to ask him to join Stoen's "Legion", a flowery word that he put on there to make his little caravan sound more appealing to the average sword swinger. Creighton was promised plenty of things; coin, land, political favor, however the thing that piqued his interest the most; a free suit of fitted armor.

As the wagon makes it to the camp, Creighton hops off the back, his bag slung over his shoulder, and his prime sword strapped to his hip, cubed pommel shining like glass. The rest of the men on the wagon hop off as well, the Cattle-Master yells back at all of them, "All you who are joining the Legion, report to the brown tent over there! Vordana, go and speak with Sir Stoen, over in the green tent!" Creighton follows his instructions, and walks toward the large green tent, looking around the camp as he goes. There are a fair number of men, and a few women, strewn across the camp, most of them donned in very simple leather or cloth armor, and several in plain clothes, likely the newcomers. *"I have seen worse armies"* Creighton thinks to himself.

Creighton approaches the entrance to the green tent, which has two men with spears and small metal shields on either side, "My name is Creighton Vordana, I am here at request of Samuel Stoen." The two guards nod, and wave him in. Creighton walks through the door flaps, and inside stands several men, of varying sizes and looks, however Samuel Stoen was easy to identify.

A true marvel of a man, Creighton admits to himself. Creighton is far from a dwarf, but even Stoen stands half a head taller than Vordana, and he is built like an ox. On his head he bears neck-length red hair, and has thick sideburns to match. Samuel's eyes are small for his head, but are a bright green that can pierce like an arrow into your ghost. His jaw is broad with a narrow chin, large ears, and a short, wide nose compliments his face.

He is adorned in his armor, which Creighton was told that he wears at all hours of the day, save when he is sleeping or cleansing himself. His armor was polished and clean, the woven leather beneath and in the joints was the green that he loved so much. Despite how nice the armor is, it has seen a fair amount of battle, and nicks and slashes were quickly buffed out, if you inspect it closely, the scars of conflict can be seen.

Stoen looks over to the entrance, "Ah, you must be Creighton Vordana. You match the description I was given, at least." Creighton nods his head, "Yes, Sir Stoen, it is I." "Excellent, you are the last one that I have been truly waiting for. I suppose introductions are in order." Stoen begins gesturing across the room, "This is Brandon Boldwood", he points to a tall and stout man with sun tanned skin, very short brown hair with long and wide sideburns, and dark blue eyes. His jaw is round, chin is square, and nose is quite tall. His dress was that of light tan hide, except for the polished iron chestplate, and a vented iron tassets hanging from his waist. On the right bicep of his jacket is the Stoen Crest, a gauntlet in a fist with two of the letter S facing each other.

Samuel points to another, "This is Yesha Monrow", a taller man with long blonde hair, wearing dark cloth armor with metal rivets, that is a green so dark it is almost black. He bears the Stoen Crest on his left shoulder. Next was Lia Benton, a shorter man with light brown hair and a high-quality looking set of custom leather armor, a style that Creighton had never seen before. It was quite tight fitting, and the pieces were stitched and riveted together in a diamond pattern, the different pieces changing color from nearly black brown, to a pale yellow, and the rivets are of a shiny gray steel He also bears the Stoen Crest, on his right pectoral.

 Last, was Joppa Jak, dressed in his standard preferred attire of choice, a light tan jacket with a white undershirt, almost as white as his body, a pair of brown pants, tanned leather short boots, and a short scarf. It is white, with thick red stitching at each end, and a crossing pattern inked in black all across it. Attached to his thigh is a quiver of short arrows, and on his back is a short bow. His Stoen Crest is actually painted onto the side of his quiver, the only man in the room to not have it on his clothing.

 "Now, Creighton, we were just in the middle of a briefing of responsibilities. So you arrived just in time. Please, set your things down, and come to the table." Creighton did just that, approaching the table, standing next to Joppa. The two of them exchange a look, nod at one another, and turn their attention to Stoen. While what Stoen speaks of was very important, Creighton cannot help but allow his mind to drift to his promised suit of armor…

It is night time once the meeting of generals has concluded, and Creighton had arrived in the late morning. Stoen stays behind in his tent while the rest are excused to eat and mingle with the others. Creighton cracks his neck with his hands, and says "I need a strong drink. Who knows where to get one?" Brandon points toward a wagonhouse over near a bonfire with his thumb, "Over there. I am going to go rest." He breaks off and heads toward the edge of the camp, "I think I could stand to join you, Creighton." says Joppa, and the two of them begin walking toward the wagonhouse.

To both of their elation, there was indeed some strong drink, thick, dark ale that is not king quality, but serves the two tired mercenaries just fine. Creighton and Joppa take seats by the bonfire, Creighton on a shaven down log, and Joppa cross legged on the ground, closer to the fire. Creighton starts off the conversation, "So, what draws you here, Joppa? Fortune, favor, rebellion?" Joppa takes a swig of his drink, "I am far from my rebellious years. No, I have come here for the same reason as most of the men here carrying swords over spears, reward. I have been promised a plot of land anywhere I wish, as well as a nice box of coin, if this little rebellion goes well. How about yourself? I can tell by your attire that you are not a simple farmer who is putting hope in a new king."

Creighton nods, "You would be correct. I was asked to join by messenger, sent from Stoen himself apparently. Ever since I left my previous job at arms, I have been doing paid sword work. Apparently, those two things made Stoen interested in me. I suppose I should be honored, eh?" Creighton takes a swig of his drink, "And yes, I joined for the same reason as yourself. My pockets could stand to be a bit heavier. Also I am looking forward to that set of armor. However, a piece of land seems nice as well. I may bargain for that as well…"

"If I may ask, what was your previous job at arms? Was it for Drow?" Joppa asks, looking at the fire, "No, not Drow. Outside of the Lockhart territory, up north. I spent a year as a charge soldier, went through a few promotions, and eventually I decided to move on south. Did not think I would end up in service to another king, or prospective king in this instance, but what can I say? A man needs his coin." Joppa nods, "Was it the Resettle Territory?" "No, further east, the Markall Territory. Why?" Creighton responds, "My sister is up in the Resettle area, that is all. I do not know much about the Markall Territory, what is it like?"

Before Creighton can respond, he is interrupted by the sound of commotion a short way across the camp. Lia Benton has one of the new recruits by the collar, berating him up close in his face. Creighton and Joppa both take notice, as Lia snatches a small bag from the young man's hand and shoves him to the ground. Lia upends the bag, spilling what appears to be dried meat onto the man's head, and then tosses the bag into one of the smaller fires next to him. "Any idea what that is about?" Creighton asks Joppa. Joppa nods, "Yes. That poor soldier showed up yesterday, dropped off by his parents to fight for Stoen."

Lia steps on the young man's stomach, continuing to berate him from above, "Lia has a tendency to try and 'weed out the weak ones', which is his way of saying that he enjoys swinging around his rank and tormenting the newcomers." Creighton stands up, realizing his cup has gone dry, "He seems like quite the gentleman." he says sarcastically. Joppa shakes his head, "Not the word I would use…"

Chapter #7

The leaves have begun to brown again in the town of Stonewater, this is only Creighton II's second autumn. Tanta is sitting under the shade of a tree in her favorite red casual gown, her maroon, woven hair cloth, watching as young Creighton plays in the leaves. Since his first, the boy has seemed to love the autumn, he enjoys the crunchy leaves and the active wildlife. Tanta loves watching her son at play, it fills her heart with warmth, as he laughs and capers.

Tanta looks up into the sky, it is beginning to turn pink with the setting of the sun. It is a day much like that day, Tanta remembers it vividly. The sky was much like it is now, Tanta was leaning out of the window of the kitchen, looking up to the clouds when they arrived, Stoen's Legion. That was a terrible day, but not all bad, as it was the day she met her husband.

Suddenly Tanta is pulled back into modern reality, by a tugging of her sleeve, "Ma, food" the young Creighton says to Tanta, looking into her eyes. Creighton II is almost tall enough to look straight into his mother's eyes when she sat on the ground. "Oh yes, of course my son." Tanta stands and gives her son a light underhanded wave, gesturing for him to follow. "Let us return home, and we will get something to eat."

Tanta and Creighton II begin walking home, Tanta going slowly so young Creighton can stay by her side. "The faster we go, the faster you can eat, my son." Creighton II, being the hungry young child he is, hears his mother's words and begins to walk as fast as he can. Tanta quickens her pace into a light jog to keep up with the boy. Tanta smiles, looking down at her son, hustling as fast as his body will allow. Suddenly his own feet betray him and he falls to the dirt with a thud.

Tanta stops next to him and crouches down, more amused than concerned about her son's fall, "Are you alright my son?" Creighton II pushes himself up to all fours, "Yesh" he says confidently, at least as confident as a child his age can be. As he stands, Tanta sees his right leg. It must have been caught on a rock, as there is a large, openly bleeding cut in the middle of his right shin. "Oh my" Tanta exclaims, "Come here my son, I will carry you home." The boy is confused for a moment, then looks down at his left leg, then his right. He sees the cut, but does not react. Tanta scoops the boy up in her arms and carries him toward their home.

Creighton I is standing out front of his home, he has a dead hare on a table. Creighton picks up his knife and rolls the hare onto its back, grabs the hare by its hind legs and presses the knife to its lower belly, he slides it down, cutting the skin and into the flesh. Butchering and skinning, while not completely new to Creighton, is something that he has minimal experience in. Normally, he merely field-dresses the animals, rarely has he actually butchered the animals for cooking.

He grew up in a military family, and lived a military life up until the last few years. Creighton has been a hunter and tracker since he was young, but his job was always to retrieve the animals and finish them if they still breathed. His Brother, Reh, was the Archer of the family and his sister was the one to prepare it. However Creighton has been practicing with the bow, although not making much progress, and he has decided it was time he learned to properly prepare an animal for eating.

Start with a hare, then maybe a hog, and go from there. *"Next, take the legs off"* he thinks to himself. Creighton places the knife against the leg of the hare, and realizes he is not quite sure where to cut it. Before he can decide, he hears a voice "Hello Creighton." Creighton looks over his shoulder, it is Tanta, carrying their son. Creighton sees the bloody leg, "What happened to the boy?"

Tanta walks in through the front door of their home, "He fell and sliced his leg on a rock." Creighton stabs his knife into the table he was using for the hare, "Ah, the scars of childhood." Creighton walks inside behind her, "He will be fine. I cut myself many times, many ways when I was his age." Tanta sits Creighton on their eating table and retrieves her box of treatment supplies. Creighton looks down at his son, "So my son, what did you learn from this?" Creighton II looks up at his father, and simply shrugs. "Watch your footing. Today it was your knee, another day it may be your eye, or your neck. Watch where you walk." Creighton II nods his head, as Tanta sits down to his left.

Tanta begins with pouring a clear liquid onto the wound, a concoction called helda, made of mostly fermented grain and basil. Tanta pours some on an old cloth, and begins to dab at the bleeding leg of the boy. Creighton II does not make a sound, not a wince or a whine, to both of the parents' surprise. Tanta looks up to Creighton the First, "Well, he truly is as tough as his father." Creighton smiles at the comment, then returns outside to continue the butchering of the hare.

Creighton closes the door behind him, and returns to the table at which he worked. Before he can pull the knife from the wood however, he overhears a conversation between a man and his wife, from across the road. "Dogs?" the man says to the woman, "Yes, from what I had heard. Tearing up a whole village, no one left." The man shakes his head, "That is a shame. Stoen needs to get his men on that. I have said many times we have too many wolves around here! But they have never taken any kind of action."

Creighton's ears perked at the conversation, curious. Are they only talking about the wolves? He heard no mention of generals or beheadings. So maybe that part of the story was still unknown. Still, the mention of it made him somewhat uneasy. Creighton had somewhat made the attempt to flush that letter from his mind, but it still troubled him here over a year later. Thankfully however, there was no further word from King Stoen, so hopefully things were going better, despite what he had just heard. But hopes are not something to be relied on...

Creighton proceeds to butcher the hare, thinking back to how his mother did it when he was a boy. He finishes the process, and is left with a fairly good looking piece of meat, if not a little sloppy, Creighton thought to himself. Creighton takes the hare on the slab into the house, pulling the door closed behind him, "Tanta, it is ready to be prepared." Tanta is sitting next to Creighton II on the floor, he is playing with a forest cat carved of wood. She stands up and looks onto the slab at the hare, "It looks good, thank you much, my love." Tanta takes the slab from Creighton and turns toward the fireplace.

"While I was outside, I had a thought. I think I am going to take a trip to Hikline soon." Tanta looks over her shoulder at Creighton, "Oh. Why is that?" "In all honesty, I was thinking about the letter from Stoen. It said not to go to Lockhart, or to speak on the matter publicly. However, I believe there is someone there who I may be able to speak to regarding this situation, someone who knows a lot of things, and may be able to provide some unbiased information. If nothing else,

I can confirm what I have already heard." Tanta nods, "That may be good. The more we can know about all this, the better." Creighton nods, "It has been a while since I saw Hikline, anyhow."

Tanta turns and gives Creighton a kiss on his cheek, "Do whatever you feel that you need to. Now, I will begin cooking. You relax." Creighton thumbs his eye, scratching it, then walks over to his bed and sits on the edge, grabbing a book from the end table. It is titled "Lives of Lordship", it is a detailed cataloging of the various rulers from the different territories. Their lives, failures, accomplishments, and deaths, stretching back almost five hundred years. While Creighton is only a few pages in, the information inside is riveting.

Obviously, it does not contain the end of Drow or the start of Stoen, however it does contain Drow's beginning. Creighton had a morbid curiosity about the life of the king that he helped end. Drow had the most unusual rise to power, as he was not a member of the ruling family, but also not of any great political standing. The king before him, as well as *his* family, and many members of the civilian population, had all died of the same disease. Which could have been avoided, however they were a superstitious group of people, who refused any form of medicine. The reason for that is greatly debated, however the most popular thought is that they were afraid of being poisoned.

Drow was essentially elected into the position, which he accepted somewhat begrudgingly. He had no wife, and no children, however he had an adopted boy that he raised as his Great Auxiliary, which is essentially the second in command and advisor to the King. Creighton actually remembers seeing the Great Auxiliary, a strange young fellow, with odd hair, during the siege of Lockhart. But, like his king, he is dead now. The king who preceded Alestin Drow was Kegg Arandro, who was born into power, taking the kingship at age twenty.

Before that, a man named Cessal Arandro, father of Kegg, who died of natural causes at the age of one hundred and thirty. Before Cessal was a queen named Landet Arandro, mother of Cessal, as well two others. She was the only queen of Lockhart in the last three hundred years. Landet was known for being very shrewd and strict, but not necessarily cruel. Then there are all the various kings and queens outside the Lockhart Territory. Creighton is well-schooled on the royal lineage from the Markall Territory, of course.

As Creighton is reading, he feels something grabbing at the cuff of his boot. He looks down, and it is Creighton II, with a smile on his face. *"What a huge child..."* the father thinks to himself with a hint of pride. "Yes, boy?" He asks, as he sets his book down, and reaches down to grab his son up under the arms. Creighton sets his son down next to him, "Are you wanting to read this?" He waves the book in front of the child. Creighton II grabs the book in both hands, looks at it for a moment, then slowly brings it forward and taps it against his forehead.

This gets a hearty laugh from Tanta, "My son, that is not quite how it works." Creighton takes the book and pulls his son up next to his side. "Here, I will do it for you." Creighton opens the book to the first chapter on Royalty of the Markall Territory, "The Markall Territory, this is where your father is from." He says to Creighton II. "You were born in the Lockhart Territory, correct?" Creighton asks Tanta, "Yes, not too far from Lockhart itself." she answers. "Excellent, that was what I thought. Now, the Markall Territory, my son..."

Creighton II reaches out and touches the page with his fingers, "Oh, you wish to start with King Wendell? Then that is where we shall begin. King Darios Wendell was the sixth king of the Markall Territory. When he was twenty-eight, he won the throne in a duel against the previous king, Revid Estenmell. The two fought with short daggers, and they battled from dusk until dawn, when King Estenmell finally collapsed from his wounds, and allowed Darios Wendell to take the throne, as well as control over the territory. King Wendell was famous in his Territory, and infamous in others, for his strongarm trade deals and fierce protection of the pride and sanctity of the territory."

Creighton turns the page, "He bore six children, three sons and three daughters, however his first daughter did not live for long outside of the womb. The ones who survived were Astoia, who was the oldest son, Grendal, who was the oldest daughter, a pair of twin boys named Jeka and Keja, and the youngest of them all as Yamoya, King Wendell's final daughter. Darios Wendell lived to be sixty-eight, and died of a cold-borne illness. Astoia was supposed to take the kingship from his father, however was killed during a drunken fight the night of the funeral, which he instigated, and escalated by brandishing a weapon. So the Kingdom went to Grendal."

Tanta pipes in, "And that did not work out so well, from what I remember." Creighton shakes his head, "Correct. After a measly three months of her queenship, she was assassinated. There were several reasons, the biggest likely being the taxes, as in one day she doubled what the civilians were expected to pay. She took a shredding arrow to the abdomen, and died later that evening, she was barely missed by even her own siblings. After that, the twins took over the territory together, and ruled side by side until their deaths, when the son of Jeka took over. The current king of the Markall Territory is a man named Pratius Mashor, a very bold and strong man. A man that your father once served." Creighton says, looking down at his son.

Tanta looks over to the two Creighton's, "What ever did bring you down out from the Markall Territory anyhow, my love?" Creighton does not respond for a moment, "Just some personal business, and I had decided that it was time to move along. Lockhart seemed as good of a place as any." Tanta turns back to her cooking, "Does that book of yours mention the story of the Mage King?" Creighton shakes his head, "It is a history book, not a book of tales and fiction." "Well D'zech was a real person." "You believe those foolish stories?" Tanta looks at Creighton, "I do, yes. They are not foolish, they are true." Creighton rolls his eyes, "Well, even if they were, this book only goes back five hundred years. Now, I will be getting back to teaching our son *history*." Tanta nods her head and rolls her eyes, "As you will, my love."

Chapter #8

Creighton is slowly walking through the shallow snow, hunting bow in hand, a quiver on his hip, but his cape not on his back, as it often was. He had torn it the other week, and it was in need of repair. His archery skills have improved somewhat, however, still nowhere close to the likes of Joppa. Creighton is following some deer tracks that seemed fresh in the shallow snow. The winter has been quite mild so far, in fact this was the first snowfall of the year, which was normally the heaviest of the season in this part of the country. So the people are expecting this winter to be quite the easy one.

Trailing a small distance behind Creighton is Gesa, who had kindly asked Creighton to take him hunting. While he was not excited at the prospect, he thought maybe Gesa may learn something, and he could make the boy carry whatever they killed. "Creighton, we have been out here for quite some time. Are you sure that we are following the tracks correctly?" Creighton looks over his shoulder at the boy, "How do you propose, that one can follow tracks wrongly?" Gesa opens his mouth, then closes it without saying anything. "Now, be quiet unless it is absolutely needed. If you must talk, speak more softly. The animals are dumb, but not deaf."

With that, the two of them continued on. The sun is beginning to rise, the dark early morning sky beginning to be broken by a deep orange, creeping past the clouds. Creighton has let his hopes drop, it seems that the deer that had made these tracks were long gone. The time out in the woods has been nice, however. Creighton has always been a fan of the winter, despite the harsh conditions that can arise from it. When it is nice and mild, like this, it is quite pleasant. As well as the pleasure of coming inside from the cold, and sitting by a fire, and having a hot meal. Especially as a young child.

As Creighton is contemplating telling Gesa that it is time to return to home, he sees something in the distance, a large black bird, with a bright red head, walking out of some brush. Gesa sees it too, and gets excited. Creighton quickly puts his hand back and touches Gesa on the chest, "Do not speak" Creighton says in a hushed whisper. They crouch down and slowly start to get closer, the bird does not notice and begins sifting through the snow, looking for something to eat. Once they get within, what Creighton considers, arrow range, the two of them stop. Creighton kneels down, pulls an arrow, and nocks it.

Creighton pulls up the bow and takes aim at the bird, then takes a deep breath... This is the first time he has attempted to shoot a live animal in his adult life. Creighton aims at the body of the bird, and releases the arrow. It flies, and strikes the bird flush in the side, knocking it down, and it begins to flop and convulse. *"Excellent shot"* Creighton says to himself, before standing up, "Come, Gesa". The two of them walk toward the bird, it is still shaking a little, not completely dead. Creighton pulls out a knife and goes to kneel down, then looks at Gesa and holds it out, "Here, take off the head." Gesa looks at Creighton, "Well... can we not just wait for it to die?" Creighton shakes his head, "No need to let it squirm and suffer. Besides, I am ready to get back to a fire. Now go on, take it."

Gesa timidly takes the knife from Creighton, it is a fairly large blade, with some weight to it. He walks up to the turkey and kneels down by the head, "How do I do it?" Creighton points to the head, "Grip it just under the head with your empty hand, and press the knife to the base of the neck. Then with both speed and strength, cut back and forth until you make it through. They are fairly skinny, so it should not take but a few swipes." Gesa grabs the head of the bird and holds it still, and takes a few breaths, then takes the knife, and quickly begins to cut through the neck.

The turkey lets out a squawk, and after a few seconds of vigorous sawing, the head is disconnected, and the bird lets out one last little shake, before becoming completely limp. Gesa has some blood on his hand, which seems to upset him a bit, and Creighton notices. He holds out his hand for the knife, "Have you never killed an animal before, Gesa?" Gesa hands him the bloody knife and shakes his head, and so does Creighton, "What *has* your father taught you, boy?" Gesa wipes the blood off his hand on the side of his boot, "Not a lot of things, sir." Creighton takes a handful of snow and wipes it down the blade of his knife, cleansing the blood off. *"No wonder why he is constantly coming to me with questions..."* he thinks.

"Well, now we shall have fresh meat tonight. Is that not an enticing thought?" Gesa smiles a little, "Yeah, that does sound nice. However, tonight Lum told me that I could join her family for a meal this evening." Creighton gives Gesa a sly look and a smirk, "Well, good for you, Gesa. That girl seems to have taken quite the liking to you, has she not? Grab the bird by the legs, you are carrying it." Gesa grabs the bird and the two of them start walking back toward Stonewater, "I suppose she has. She is very..." "Pretty?" Creighton interjects. Gesa puts his head down, "Well, yes. That as well. I was going to say, strong, and kind."

Creighton chuckles, "Kind was not the word that came to my mind when she was throwing you around like a wolf with a hare." Gesa looks at Creighton, "That was just, how she shows her affection, I guess." "All people do it in different ways. Some pick flowers, others engage in duels, some write songs." Creighton rolls his neck, "It almost makes me wonder if Kentra is secretly affectionate of me, seeing how Lum treats *you.*" Gesa lets out a quick laugh,

"Ha! Uh... no. I do not think so..." Creighton looks to Gesa, "I was speaking in jest, but you seem extremely confident. Have you heard things?" Gesa looks to the ground, "Well, Lum and I do spend an amount of time together, and Kentra is often around, and well..."

Creighton slaps Gesa on the shoulder, "Spit it out, boy." "She, speaks unkind things of you, in private." Creighton drapes his bow over his shoulder, "Such as?" It matters little what Kentra exactly said, however he is curious, nonetheless. Gesa does not respond for a moment, "I will not hold her words against you, boy, nor will I tell her you told me anything." That seemed to be the reassurance that Gesa needed, "Kentra says that you are venal, and a secret coward. That honorable men do not take up arms for money, and that you will not fight her, because you are scared of her." Creighton does not outwardly respond, but in his mind gets a vision of plunging his fist clear through Kentra's chest, and waving her around like a flag. "Did she say anything else?" He asks Gesa. The boy goes silent for a minute, "And that she did not know eunuchs could father children."

Creighton sharply inhales through his nose, is silent for a moment, then "Well, I am happy to know how she truly feels." Gesa looks forward again, deciding that this topic is not one he wants to continue, "So... how do *you* do it?" "Do what?" Creighton asks, "Show affection, to a woman."

Creighton thinks for a moment, then responds "I have my ways, boy. But a master craftsman never reveals all of his techniques. I will give you one piece of advice, however. Be confident in yourself. No matter your size, shape, background, or length of your manhood, no woman likes a timid, sniveling coward. You could be the most handsome and strong man to ever live, but if you are the kind who looks down at his shoes and talks poorly of himself, that is a woman deterrent." Gesa nods his head, "Understood. Thank you."

The sun has finally raised itself high into the sky, and has bathed the land in light, as Creighton and Gesa make it back to Stonewater. Creighton turns to Gesa and holds out his hand, "I will take the bird, now. I will be sure that Tanta delivers your family part of the meat." Gesa nods and hands over the bird, which Creighton throws over his shoulder, "You did a good job today, Gesa. Now head home." Gesa smiles, then turns and walks back toward his home. Creighton does the same, walking toward his home.

As Creighton approaches, he sees his son sitting on the small table outside the front door to their home, staring directly upwards. "Hello, my boy. Why are you out here?", he asks as he sets his bow down by the doorframe. "Because he wanted to look at the sky!" Tanta yells from inside the house, where the door is cracked open slightly. Creighton walks over to Creighton II, and scoops him up with his free arm, then slaps the dead bird down where the child was sitting. Creighton walks inside, son on his side, "I shot us a big bird, got it right in the vitals, I believe." Tanta looks at the two of them and clasps her hands together, "Excellent. I will begin the butchering soon."

Creighton sets his son down on the floor, who immediately runs over to his bed and climbs up onto it, with little effort. The reaching was not much of a problem, as he was a fair bit taller than other children his age. Creighton walks up to Tanta and gives her a kiss on the lips, then walks over to the hanging rack, and takes off the coat he had been wearing for his hunting. "How was it with Gesa?" Tanta asks, "The boy has pitifully little experience, in anything. I had him finish off the bird, and he acted like I was asking him to cut off his own fingers."

Tanta shakes her head, "Does his father teach him nothing?" Creighton walks over to her side, "It seems not, even the boy said so himself." Tanta looks at Creighton, "I suppose he is lucky that you are so generous, then." Creighton crosses his arms and leans on the counter top, "By the time I was his age, I was military trained and helped slaughter many animals for harvest. It is strange to see a boy so... I suppose 'innocent' would be applicable." "Well not all boys are bred into the military. The world needs poets and coopers, afterall." Tanta replies.

"I suppose that is true." Creighton looks down at himself, "Which reminds me, I must walk over to the Delgoss home, Unet said that she would be finished with the repairs on my cape today." Unet was the mother of Lum & Kentra, wife of Hatch Delgoss, and the best seamstress in the territory, or at least the town. Tanta nods and says "Alright my love, I will start on the bird. It will be a treat for tonight." Creighton nods, and walks out the door.

He leaves his home, pulling the door closed behind him and walking down the stoned road toward the home of the Delgoss family. He finds himself thinking back to the disrespect from Kentra. Their relationship has not greatly improved, the girl still likes to throw verbal jabs and little backhanded comments, actively trying to test his patience. She was lucky that Hatch had Creighton's respect, or the girl may be short a tongue... or a head.

He had always wondered if the girl would be able to fight as well as she could talk, but likely not. Large muscles do not make for a competent fighter, a mistake Creighton has seen many men make, in his time. However, Creighton has never fought a woman of her build before, maybe it would be worth just getting it out of both their systems... As he realizes what he was thinking, he reaches up and slaps himself across the cheek. *"Get a hold of yourself, Creighton, you know that would go poorly."* he thinks. Creighton rolls his shoulders as he approaches the Delgoss home, then knocks on their door. He can hear the sound of joyful chatter inside, it seemed that Hatch was divulging another one of his amusing tales.

"On the way!" yells someone from inside, Creighton crosses his arms and awaits the door to be opened. After a moment, Lum opens the door for Creighton, and the smell of wine comes to his nose fast. "Ah! The Soldier Sir, how are you this night?" Creighton looks to the sky, with the sun still shining, and looks back to Lum, "I am well. Your mother has my cape." Lum looks at Creighton blankly for a moment, then remembers how to speak "Yes! Yes-yes. Come in Creighton." Lum says as she gestures inside, he follows her into the home.

Inside, Hatch is sitting at their dining table with Unet, Kentra, and Gesa. The smell of stewed deer meat is in the air. Hatch is mid-story, "-and as was going to charge me, I dropped to the ground on my hands and knees, and the damned cat went straight off the edge!" Everyone begins to laugh, Kentra slapping the table with her palm. "So, that's why my family stopped trying to train the forest cats... Oh, hello Creighton! Here for your cape I assume." Hatch says to Creighton, as he notices his arrival.

"Indeed. If I could get it, I would be right on my way." Creighton says, arms still crossed, "Oh come now, my good sir, would you not like a glass of wine?" Hatch insists. Creighton shakes his head, "It is a little early for me to indulge in the drink, thank you." While Creighton normally would not drink until the sun was down, the truth was that he knew that sharing a table with Kentra would only result in a quarrel. Unet stands from the table "Of course. Just a moment and I will retrieve it." As Unet walks away, Lum walks over to Gesa and sits down next to him on the bench, Lum grabs the boy and pulls him into her lap. Creighton cracks a small smile at the sight, *"Good for Gesa,"* he thinks to himself.

At this time Creighton notices that Kentra is staring at him, and looks at her. "Hello Kentra. May I help you?" Kentra shakes her head gently, "No, I do not believe so." Creighton turns to face her fully, "Then why do you stare?" Kentra purses her lips and nods her head from side to side, "No reason." Creighton looks to her father, "What is wrong with the girl?" Hatch stands, "I do not know. But I am *sure*, that she will fix herself. Correct, my daughter?"

Kentra says nothing, and just looks back down to her cup. "Good girl." Hatch says with some annoyance in his voice. Unet finally returns with his cape, "Here you are my sir. All holes and tears have been patched and seamed." She hands Creighton the folded up cape, which he immediately unfolds and holds it up by the corners, inspecting it. "Fine work, as always. Thank you Unet." Creighton tosses the cape over his shoulder, "You all enjoy your meal."

He turns around to leave, "No payment?" Creighton stops and looks over his shoulder, "What?" Kentra is leaning on the table with her elbow, looking at Creighton, "My mother worked very hard to fix that for you. I think you owe her some coin." Creighton turns around, "No payment was agreed upon." Kentra stands from her seat, "Do you think that because you used to be a military man, that we are all your servants?" Hatch quickly stands "Kentra! Shut your mouth."

She ignores her father, "You were bribed to help kill the old King, and now all of us lowly dirt dwellers, who have not wielded a sword or donned armor, are around to please and benefit you. Is that what you think?" Creighton grabs the cape from his shoulder and throws it to the ground, "I know not of what demon has possessed you, girl, but I suggest that you drop the tone and know your place." At this point Kentra crosses her arms, "And where is my place, Vordana? At your feet? You think so highly of yourself, yet you are no better than any of us." Creighton storms up to Kentra, anger and death in his eyes. His chest is beating, he presses his forehead to Kentra's, staring into her eyes. No one speaks, no one moves, Lum is holding Gesa tightly.

A few moments pass... Creighton looks at Hatch, then at Unet, then to Lum and Gesa... Creighton reaches into his coat pocket and pulls out a small purse. He takes the sack and slams it down onto the table with a metallic crash of the coins, causing those still sitting to jump slightly. "There." Creighton turns his back to Kentra, walking back to the cape that he had tossed to the ground, he bends over to pick it up. Recovering the freshly stitched cape, Creighton storms out of the home, no one else speaking a single word. Creighton is seething with anger, teeth clenched, if he had not been in Hatch's home, he may have killed the girl. He feels the itch, that horrible itch in his bones. Creighton needs to fight something, anything. He needs the feeling of breeching blood, of fighting. Something he has not done in too long.

Creighton walks right past his home, throwing his cape around his shoulders and buckling around his neck. *"I think it is time that I took that trip to Hikline."* Creighton thinks to himself, as he storms past his home, not even looking into the window. The sound of his boots hitting the ground is a deep and loud thud that can be heard by anyone nearby. Creighton's fists are clenched, walking as much with his shoulders as with his legs. This mood that Creighton is in, is not entirely uncommon, while he attempts to suppress it the best he can. When he walks like this, everybody in town knows to step aside, including Tanta.

Tanta sees him pass their home, and leans out of the doorway after he has already passed by, she sees the way that Creighton is walking, she can feel it in the air. He has the battle lust again... Tanta lets out a sigh. "He will be back, he always comes back" She whispers to herself.

Chapter #9

[Stoen's Legion]

Creighton Vordana stands above a beaten and bloody man, who is gasping for air as his mouth fills with blood, due to losing all of his front teeth, and the pressure from Creighton's boot on his chest helps not. Creighton sheaths his sword, the cubed pommel shining red with blood. "Now, as we were saying..." Creighton wipes blood off his chest plate with his hand and brings his eyes back up from the beaten man on the ground, to a shivering old man curled up against a tree, "This town is now under the dominion of Samuel Stoen. Any further questions or rebellion, will be met with the same response as this poor bastard." He flicks the blood from his gauntlet at the man on the ground, who is, or was, the Peacekeeper of the town.

Creighton looks from the man, to the rest of the townsfolk, "Is this well understood?" Surrounding the townsfolk, were other members of Stoen's legion, his army who are helping to claim territory on their way to dethrone King Drow. Many just nod their heads in approval, some speak in varying terms of "Yes Sir". Creighton takes his boot from the chest of the beaten Peacekeeper and turns to the men under his command, "You, make sure that all of the Drow banners are packed. You, check with General Benton that all the coin is seized. And you, commission a letter to General

Boldwood, informing him we have taken Fay Town." All the addressed men nod, and hurry away to fulfill their assigned duties.

"Where did Joppa get to?" Creighton wonders to himself. Stoen had paired Creighton and Joppa to take control of the same battalion, so the men under Creighton's command are also under Joppa's. While other, more prideful, men may have been annoyed, not having their own command, but neither of them minded it. But this also means that they have to both be together, before giving any marching orders. Creighton sees General Lia Benton walking out of a house, dragging a large, rope-handled box behind him. "Boys! Help me out!" he calls out to the men under his command.

Two of his charge soldiers hussle over and grab the box. As they pick it up, a young man runs at them, yelling "Stop!" Before he can breach the doorway, however, Lia kicks the young man in the chest, knocking him to his back, and Lia pulls his hatchet from his belt. "It is not worth your life, kid." The young man does not attempt to stand, and instead crawls backward, retreating into the house. Lia slips his hatchet back into his belt loop as Creighton approaches him, "Benton! Have you seen where Joppa got off to?" Lia reaches up to crack his neck with his hands, "Last I saw, he was going into the inn over there." Creighton nods, and walks over to the town inn. A nice little place, outside of the violence of this day. He kicks the door open, almost knocking it from the frame, "Joppa!" he yells as he looks inside.

Joppa Jak is kneeling down, looking into a corner, speaking to a frightened woman with two children. "You, have my most sincere condolences, madam. However, this is how change is made. Once Stoen is in place, then the blood will end, and the land will be better than it was before." Creighton slaps his gauntlet against his chest, making a loud metallic slap "Joppa! It is time for us to move on!" Creighton yells at him. Joppa lets out a light sigh, and looks over his shoulder at his friend, "Just, one, moment. I am speaking to the woman."

He looks back into the eyes of the worried woman. "It is time for us to go. You will see what I have told you is true, I assure you." Joppa reaches behind his back, and pulls a coin from his pocket. "Here", he places it on her lap, "You will need this once the old King is gone." It is a small golden coin, on one side is the carving of an armored fist, on the other is a mirrored S. This is to become the common coin of the territory, once Stoen takes over, and denounces the old currency. The woman picks up the coin and looks at it, she then looks up at Joppa and nods. He could see that she was still worried, but he also saw a glimmer of hope, or faith, in her face.

Joppa stands, and walks toward the door, "Alright my friend, now we will go." Creighton steps out of the doorway, Joppa by his side. They both walk toward a cart strapped to a bull. "You spend too much time and effort speaking to these people, Joppa." Joppa pulls one of the short-arrows from his quiver and begins to play with it, "I do not think so. For that woman, I may have made an impression on her. Many of these people, they may follow from fear or from impartiality. However she may follow, because she thinks that Stoen truly is a better fit for King."

Creighton cracks a small smirk, "Since when do you honestly care for the Stoen agenda?" Joppa, wiggling the short-arrow between his index and middle finger says "I do not. However, I find it is best for the little folk if they believe, that we believe." "Hmph, you are a kind man." Creighton responds, Joppa nods his head, "In this time of war that we are in, someone must be." As the pair approach the cart, Joppa flicks his short-arrow back down into his quiver. "Did you collect everything that we were instructed to?" he asks one of the charge soldiers in green leather boots, the boots of a Stoen soldier.

"Yes General Jak, everything we were instructed." he says with confidence. Creighton gives the cart a quick look over, looking inside of the cart itself and peeking into some of the bags hanging off the side. Weaponry, lots of coin, and the banners of the town. They have been replaced with those bearing the Stoen fist, and are the green that the man himself is so fond of. Creighton slaps the side of the wagon, "Very good. Now hit the bull and let us go." The Cattle-Master atop the wagon reaches down with his gloved hand and gives the bull a firm slap at the base of the tail, the giant animal grunts and begins walking.

Creighton and Joppa jump onto the back of the cart and sit, while the rest of the soldiers walk alongside and behind. "I pity them. I remember my days as a charge soldier, walking until my soles bled." Joppa Jak says with a slight smile, thinking back to his youth. Creighton pulls out his knife and examines the blade, checking for dents or cracks, "I do not. The walking makes you strong, making your knees like rocks and your breaths all the more deep. Aside, we earned our right to ride the wagon." "I am not saying we have not, however it is still quite tiring just to watch."

Joppa turns and puts his back to the wagon wall. He removes the quiver from his thigh and empties the contents into his lap, about fifteen short arrows. Joppa begins picking up and inspecting each one individually, turning them in his hand, dragging his eyes from the tip to the nock. Checking for any little imperfection that could hinder their performance. Creighton reaches into his satchel and pulls out a thin leather sack, it is full of salted nuts.

As Creighton begins to eat, he watches as Joppa inspects his arrows. Any little nick in the tip, Joppa pulls out the whetstone that he carries on his person at all times, and smooths it out. However sometimes, he removes the head and vanes, then snaps the shaft over his knee and tosses it off the side of the wagon. Joppa strips and breaks two arrows, and Creighton feels the need to ask, "Why do you keep snapping your arrows? Have they displeased you?" he says in a manner of jest.

Joppa does not look up from his inspection, however he answers, "If there is a crack or a splinter in the shaft, it is of no use to me." Creighton tosses a nut into his mouth, "They looked fine to me. They were straight at the least." "That is why you are not an archer, my friend." Joppa tosses the arrow he is currently holding to Creighton, who catches it. "Inspect that, look closely, all around it." Joppa orders Creighton.

Creighton begins to inspect the arrow, looking up and down, rolling it in his fingers as he has seen Joppa do many times. "It, seems to be a regular shot-arrow. What of it?" Joppa touches the fingernails of his right hand to the underside of his chin, "Look closer." Creighton rolls his eyes and then squints at the arrow, "Do you see that small, modest split up the side of the shaft, about the length of my thumb." Creighton nods, "Yes, however I fail to see how that makes the arrow no good."

Creighton hands the arrow back to Joppa, "As of now, it is not. However, what if the next time I shoot it, it breaks into the target? Or if I fall on my leg, and that little split is enough to cause the arrow to snap? Now I am short one arrow during battle, or amidst a hunt." Joppa says, "I would rather have five perfect arrows than twenty sub-standard, because I know that those five would not fail me." Joppa dislodges the head from its resting place, "Besides-" Joppa begins to carefully pull the vanes, "-I take utmost pride in my equipment." Joppa pockets the head and vanes, snaps the shaft over his knee, then tosses it over his shoulder out of the wagon. Creighton shrugs his shoulders, "I suppose I would not be fit for the life of an archer. My father always taught me to use things until they broke, then get a new one."

 "Is that why you had so many mothers?" Joppa says with a smirk, Creighton gives Joppa a mildly annoyed look, and tucks his bag of nuts back into his satchel. "Generals! We have a gathering in the road ahead!" the Cattle-Master yells from his position. Creighton's ears perk and he stands up in the back of the wagon, however he can not see much from his position. Creighton gestures to Joppa, and the two of them hop off the rear of the wagon, "Cease!" Joppa calls out, and the Cattle-Master brings the bull to a stop, as well as the following soldiers of Stoen. The two Generals meet at the front of the cart, and indeed a short distance away, there is a group of people kneeling in the road. Creighton nods toward Joppa, "Your eyes are better than mine, can you make out much more?" Joppa shakes his head.

 Creighton looks over his shoulder and waves to the cart to follow, "Slowly. We will lead." Creighton and Joppa begin walking toward the large group, the rest of the legion following slowly behind. As the pair approach the group, Joppa signals over his shoulder for the carevan to stop. Creighton shakes his head as he realizes who these people are... The Brey. Creighton takes the lead "In the name of Samuel Stoen, disperse from the road." He receives no response, not even a glance. The Brey are sitting in a large circle, three rows deep, something in the center.

 "Are you all of empty ear?" calls out Joppa. One man in the center of the circle stands, he is completely nude and bald. "I apologize, sirs." His voice sounds old and dusty, he turns around, Joppa and Creighton both cringe slightly. He is quite old and pale, as well as skinny, and not a single hair could be seen on his body, from his head to his feet. The most upsetting thing, was not that they could see the man's privates, but the lack thereof. Between his legs was one giant scar, with a small hole near the top. The rumors were true, it seemed... "I, apologize, if we are impeding your travels. However, we can not move at this moment." the eunuch calls out to Creighton.

 "Why is that?" The old man turns around and looks down at what they are all gathered around. Creighton moves up to the toes of his boots, however cannot see what they are gathered around. Creighton shakes his head, "I understand not these people." Joppa looks at Creighton, "No one does. I doubt they understand themselves... they are not in the proper mind." Creighton looks to the man in the center, "I am in little mood for interruptions, especially by your... whatever it is you are doing."

Creighton places his hand on his sword, "I suggest you move, before we move you." Joppa looks at him, "So quick to the blade." Creighton looks back, "I have no interest in waiting, or in interrogating these self-mutilating madmen." There is a heavy sigh, "Brey, it is time, we disperse. Rise." says the old eunuch. All the men and women in the group rise to their feet. All of them are clad in small white ribbons and strips of white cloth, if anything at all. The Brey walk through and around the caravan, like water passing through a tree branch. Creighton grips his sword tightly, pulling it a bit out of the sheath. While the Brey are considered mad, they are also said to be harmless. It is still better to be safe, however.

Joppa can not help but to look at the people as they pass by. There are more men with the same scarring as the man from before, in fact it seemed that all full grown men were the same. The women have giant cauterization scars where their breasts would be. A truly odd and disturbing sight to behold. As the last of the Brey pass by the caravan,

Creighton waves for the caravan to follow. Creighton looks back to where they were gathered around, and in the road is a dirt rat, laying on its side. After a moment, he sees the small creature stand up to its hind legs, look around, then sprint into the woods. He shrugs, *"Worshipping rodents?"* he wonders.

As the cart passes by them, Creighton and Joppa hop back onto the back, "So they do that to themselves?" Joppa asks Creighton, who responds with a shrug, "If the stories are to be believed, and I do not question them." "But, why?" Joppa is befuddled and a slight bit concerned, "Do I appear to be the grand priest of The Brey? I know little more than you do, my friend. However, what I do know is that I do not like them. They are... too odd for my comfort." Joppa shakes his head, "I agree with you there. I cannot help but wonder what would drive a man to take a knife to his own body in that way. Whatever god they follow must be quite persuasive." "I know not if they even follow a god, at least as we think of them. I have heard several stories, but no mention of a deity."

The Brey have been rumored to possess some sort of mage-like abilities, however Creighton does not believe it. Mages and magic are little more than hear-say and myth. Afterall, Creighton has lived thirty years, seen four territories, and never seen any real magic...

-

Creighton wakes with a jolt, as the wagon he was sleeping on comes to a sudden stop. It is now dark, save the moon and various fires around the camp. Creighton sits up, Joppa is no longer on the wagon with him. As he begins to shake himself awake, he slaps himself on the chin, Creighton knows that he can not go speak with Stoen with sleep still in his eyes. He hops from the back of the wagon and stretches his arms, then walks toward the center of the makeshift encampment.

Around him soldiers are bathing, up-keeping their equipment, or cooking food. Some deer flesh hit Creighton's nostrils and suddenly he realized that those two handfuls of nuts were far from enough food for him. But that would have to wait, as the real hand-that-feeds is awaiting, the self-proclaimed King that Creighton serves. As Creighton went to approach the opening of the tent, out came General Boldwood, looking none-too pleased.

"Boldwood?" Creighton exclaims, "Are you not supposed to be in Tall Hill?" General Boldwood blows past Creighton, "There are many things that are *supposed* to be, Creighton." Boldwood charges into a tent, and suddenly there is a loud crash, like a table being thrown. Creighton is a little confused, however, Boldwood's attitude was little of his concern. Creighton approaches Samuel Stoen's tent, adjusts his belt and removes his cape, before breaching the entrance.

Inside stands Joppa Jak, Lia Benton, and the man himself, Samuel Stoen. Samuel looks over to Creighton as he enters, "Ah, Vordana." he says with his deep, naturally commanding voice, "Come, Jak was in the process of telling me of your objective today." Creighton enters the tent with his cape on his arm, Joppa continues to speak. "We were met with mild resistance, however it was of no issue. Their Peacekeeper was an older man with virtually no combat experience, at least from what we could see. Creighton loosened his teeth with little trouble. While he was doing that, and ensuring that there was no more resistance in the community, I spoke with the common folk. We suffered no casualty on our part, save a few minor wounds."

Samuel puts his hand down on the table, "Good, that is very good to hear. My banners were placed?" Creighton nods his head, "Yes sir, and the old ones were torn down and brought with us." "Excellent. I will be making a bed with all these banners once we are done, haha!" Samuel declares in a jovial voice. He was pleased, this takeover of his was going very well. His banner hung in the majority of the western and southern towns in the territory, and all Drow's men that they encountered were cut down, or put out of fighting shape at the least.

To be fair to those men, it was usually thirty to forty of them, versus sixty to one hundred of Stoen's swords. War had been absent for so long in these areas of Oblitus, it was almost surprising that there were *that* many men in these towns. Samuel slaps his hand down on the table, his metal glove making quite a loud clang, "So, which of you men is hungry? I am in the mood for deer!" Samuel strides past Creighton, Joppa and Lia. The three follow Stoen out of the tent, ready to feed themselves after this long day

Chapter #10

The morning sun shines through the window of the inn that he arrived at last night, hitting Creighton Vordana directly in his resting eyes, and waking him. His eyes crack open, and consciousness comes flooding to him like a dam had been broken. Creighton sits up in the bed, and swings his legs over the side, he begins to rub the sleep from his eyes. Memories of his time in the Stoen campaign had overtaken his dreams, Creighton shakes his head *"I had not thought of The Brey in quite some time..."* he thinks to himself.

Creighton stands from the edge of the bed, stretching his nude body, in the musty private room that he had acquired for his stay. The smell of mildew from the linens and old wood from the walls gave the place a light stink, but also a bit of a homey feel. He begins to dress himself in the same clothes that he had arrived in the previous evening. It has been three days since he had left Stonewater, and he had only arrived at his destination late last night. However, it is well worth the trip to Creighton, he has arrived in a town known as Hikline. A fairly large farming town, much larger than Stonewater for sure, the population may be around one thousand. However, despite being a farming town, they are not best known for potatoes and onions, not at all, but for the town's *other* attraction; their Lea.

The Hikline Lea is the most revered of all the fighting arenas in the entire Lockhart Territory. While it is not the only Lea in the land, it is considered the most entertaining and often the most violent. They allow many that other Leas do not, including man battling beasts, men battling women, as well as allowing all who wish to compete into the battlegrounds, regardless of qualification, age (to a degree), or sex. As far as the townsfolk and those running the Lea are concerned, allowing all comers keeps it interesting, and brings in more out-of-town audiences.

Creighton is no stranger to the Lea, however, that is not the purpose of his trip this time, although he may pay a visit while he is in town. As a spectator. Creighton walks down to the greeting area of the inn, smelling the morning meal that was cooking in the dining area. It is the usual meal that they cooked; Goose eggs, potatoes, and onions, all stirred up together and served with a side of bread. It is a fair sized inn, with plenty of standing room. Truth be told, it is as much of a drinkery as it is an inn, making it the most popular place for travelers visiting the city, especially those looking to make names for themselves in The Lea. The interior of the inn is all wood, but not all of it the same. Most of the walls and floor are identical, dark brown wood, however over the years, pieces here and there have been replaced, and the owner could not be bothered to make sure it was all matching. On the floors were the same orange and black carpets that had been there since the place was built, and they certainly look like they had.

Creighton sits down at a table and waves to the woman cooking the food, she sees him and slaps some of the food onto a plate for him. As she begins to walk over she says "Ah Vordana! It been a time. Here for t'e Lea I would guess?" Creighton looks at the woman as she sets his plate down. Renda Kep, the owner of this particular inn, "The Q" as she called it. Why she chose that name is a mystery to everyone. She is an elderly woman, around one hundred and ten years old, but she does not look a day over one hundred and fifty.

She is wrinkled, her hair a light grey, she has bumps all over her hands and some upon her face. Renda's nails are long, ending at a round tip, and she is not very tall. She walks around The Q in a grey, short sleeved dress, with a red vest, which is covered in pockets from collar to hem, the pockets are full of things from coins, to spices, to random items she finds laying on the tables. On her feet are a pair of rope sandals that look to be as old as she is, and had soaked up all manner of things from mud, to spilled ale, to blood. However what Renda lacks in youth, she makes up for in spirit. She is a witty old woman, and is plenty capable of putting down most any drunken troublemaker that decides to pester her inn.

All that, and she is the most well-informed woman in the city, from guests speaking with her, to Renda partaking in a fair bit of eavesdropping. If there is anything worth knowing in Hikline, or the Lockhart Territory as a whole, Renda is the one to consult with.

"Not this time, Renda." Creighton replies to her question and begins to eat, "Ah, t'at is a s'ame t'en. I was t'inking I would be t'rowing some coin into t'e sack after all!" Creighton smirks, "I hope you intended to bet upon me." he says in jest, she slaps him in the side of the neck "A'course I woulda! You t'e first man I ever seen beat down a wolf in t'ere! Aside, wit' t'e husban' gone, I got some coin to t'row around again." Creighton looks up at Renda "Den is dead? I am sorry to hear." Renda turns around and waves dismissively over her shoulder, "MAH! Do not be." she says as she turns her back to walk away, however Creighton grabs her wrist quickly.

"Before you go, Renda, I was wondering if I could get a private audience with you. Today." Renda turns around to face him, "Really, Creighton? And I thought you were a married man. Ha!" Creighton takes a quick look around, "This is of no laughing matter." Renda touches all her fingers together and presses them against one-another, causing them to pop and crack loudly. "Oh fine! But I got many hungry peoples here. Finis' your food t'en go wait in t'e back for me." With that, she walks off, and leaves

Creighton to his meal, which he gladly finishes.

-

Over an hour has gone by since Creighton went in the back and began waiting for Renda to finish her inn duties. While he sits there, his mind wanders, one of the places it goes is to his old suit of armor, that he received as his "bonus" for joining Stoen's Legion. A good, solid suit of armor is the best protection that a man on the battlefield could ever hope for. Like a shield for your entire body, and equally as important, there is not a woman alive who does not love a man in armor.

A woman in armor, however, seemed to scare men away. Crieghton has seen a few armor-bearing ladies in his time, mostly back in the Markall Territory, and he was never intimidated by them, himself. Quite the opposite, even when he was little more than a spear-bearing charge soldier. So much the opposite in fact, that he may have gotten in trouble... Creighton is pulled back into reality by the voice of Renda, "SO!" she exclaims as she throws the door open, pulling Creighton violently out of his own mind, "W'at did ya want?"

Creighton stands from his chair and closes the door behind her. "You know most everything that is going on in the territory, do you not?" Renda smiles, "I can tell you t'e fat'er to every bastard t'e city." Creighton raises his eyebrows, "That is good to know, I suppose." He gestures to the table in the room, Renda walks over and takes the chair, Crighton sits in the stool on the other side of the table. Renda kicks her feet up on the edge of the table, "W'at is t'is about?"

Creighton leans on the table, "I received a letter from King Stoen a short while ago. Regarding wolf attacks, on former generals from his Legion. The details were sparse, and he told me not to spread word, however-" "You know I already knew about it." Renda interjects, Creighton nods. "Yes, I have heard word of suc' t'ings. W'at do you want to know?" "Anything you can tell me." Renda uses her pinky nail to dig in her nose, "Well. For first, it is obvious t'at Stoen does not want people speaking of t'ese t'ings. I know of at least four people who have spoken about t'ese attacks and been arrested. One in town. Told t'at t'ey are attempting to disturb t'e peace. MAH! More like attempting to speak unapproved trut's."

"Have there been any survivors that have come forth?" Creighton asks, and Renda shakes her head. "Not a one. All dead. And how Stoen be acting about t'ese happenings, he probably would have t'em executed if t'ey did." Creighton rubs his chin, "Do you know who is leading these wolves? Thc beheadings suggest that there is more than just the dogs." "Ey, t'at is true! But no, nobody. Stoen and his Great Auxiliary have both been looking for answers personally, but no man, woman, or c'ild has been fingered as the culprit. T'ere have been, eh, t'irty or so people arrested in suspicion, but none were t'e one leading t'e pack." Creighton leans back in his stool, thinking deeply. "I will let you know, t'ere was one general who received his letter and fled to Lockhart, to seek protection from Stoen. He was given a place to sleep, and t'e next day, was found wit' his head taken from his s'oulders."

This was very surprising to Creighton, "Anot'er general, 'e left t'e Lockhart Territory, went west to the Mildrea Territory. It is said t'at he was in t'at territory for a day, before he was found in an inn, body bitten up and head taken off. And everyone else in the inn had been ravaged by wolves as well. Not, a, survivor. One t'ing be clear; whoever t'is wolf leader is, he is efficient, and can get places t'at most people cannot." Creighton takes a deep breath, "This is very troublesome. How can someone do something of this magnitude, without leaving a trace?" Renda strokes her chin, as a man strokes his beard, pondering. "Could be more t'an one."

Creighton had not considered that, but quickly dismisses it. "No, I do not believe so. I spent much of my youth in armies and bands, and if there were a group of people attempting to do something like this, someone would have left something incriminating, or made some sort of mistake. It is most likely one man." Creighton goes to stand up, "I must go and think." Before he can move, Renda speaks up, "There is one rumor t'at has gone around." Creighton stops to listen.

"Some say t'at t'is is the work of a King Drow loyalist. I did not t'ink t'at t'ere were any of t'ose left, but eh, I have heard it from several people."

"King Drow..." Creighton thinks. He has not heard of someone fighting for the dead king in several years. If this was the case, that may be indicative of a bigger issue... Creighton turns and begins walking away, "Thank you for your time." He walks past Renda, "One last t'ing." she says, Creighton stops again. "How is t'e boy?" she asks with a smirk.

Chapter #11

Tanta is sitting at her table, with her son, Creighton II, laying in the bed next to her, a small fire going to keep the house warm. Young Creighton is sprawled out, in nothing more than his undergarment, asleep like the dead. She thought he looked quite cute, in his current state. Looking at him, Tanta wishes that she could experience such deep, restful sleep.

While her husband's departure was quite sudden, Tanta has been enjoying the alone time with her son. It has been quieter, and Tanta has had more time to think, whenever her son was not grabbing her leg or begging for food. For his age he is quite adventurous and independent, always wanting to go outside and do things himself, even if they are the most menial tasks. He dislikes being carried, or even being lifted into his bed.

He will make a fine knight someday, Creighton and Tanta had agreed. If Stoen is still in power when the boy comes of age, they were both sure that he would gladly accept Creighton II into his service. Creighton wishes to train their son on how to wield a sword as early as reasonably possible, and Tanta sees no problem with that. Even if he does not become a knight or the like, learning to wield a sword will be a quite useful skill, and it will give both the boy and his father something to bond over.

While Tanta is sitting at the table, she has all of Creighton I's weapons and such spread across the tabletop, a rag with cleaning concoction in one hand, wiping and polishing the blade of his prime sword. She thought that, not only does this give her something productive to do while inside her warm home, but it will also be a nice surprise for when Creighton returns home. This was not the first time that he had gotten into "a mood" and stormed out of town, Tanta is used to it by now, whereas at first it worried her greatly. However, he always returns within a week or so, and always with a greatly improved demeanor.

As Tanta is polishing the blade, doing her best to make it shine, she begins to wonder what it was like to actually use a sword. Her whole life, she has never had to wield one, nor was even taught casually. Tanta sets the polishing rag down and stands from her seat, holding Creighton's sword in her right hand. She attempts to hold it out straight, but it is a little heavy. She uses her other hand and grips the handle with all her fingers, pointing it out straight in front of herself. Tanta pulls the sword back a little and takes a dainty swing with it, then again the other way. A smile creeps across her face.

Tanta raises the sword above her head and does a chopping motion down, however she does not have quite enough control, and accidentally strikes the table with the edge of the blade, making a dull, deep chop sound as the metal impacts the wood. A look of surprise hits Tanta's face as she sucks air through her teeth. She looks over her shoulder, and the young Creighton has not moved. Tanta breaths a small sigh of relief, then picks the sword back up, examining the damage to their table. Thankfully, there was little in the way of power from Tanta, so the mark in the table is shallow. Creighton's prime sword saw no wear from this, except for a little bit of scuff.

Tanta grabs the polishing cloth again and rubs the scuff off, leaving it as clean as it was when Creighton got it. Tanta starts gathering all the weapons and such from the table, and placing them back in the cupboard where they belong. *"I should take a little walk, before Creighton wakes up for dinner"* Tanta thinks, as she places the prime sword in the cupboard, and closes the doors gently. She walks over to the door and slips on a pair of simple, fur-lined hide boots. Normally, she would gladly go bare, but there was a little too much snow on the ground outside for comfort.

Tanta walks out of the house, it is evening in Stonewater, and the sun is beginning its descent into the night. Tanta's favorite time of the day, when the air really begins to cool, and the sky turns all different shades of beautiful colors. Tanta begins walking down the street, staring at the sky, and humming herself a little song. Creighton was not a fan of music, but Tanta had always loved it. Especially back when she worked in the Red Castle in Lockhart. Every month, Drow would have musicians come in and play for him and everyone in the castle.

Her time in the castle kitchens feels like multiple lifetimes ago, now, even though it was only a few years. Despite how nice it was, Tanta does not miss it too dearly. She always knew that she wanted to be a mother, some day. Once her son is of a good age, Tanta intends to ask Creighton for another, in fact. Three, that feels like the ideal number to Tanta. Hopefully two boys and one girl, however she would not be upset about having two girls and a boy. But three boys would be a slight disappointment, Tanta thinks, but of course she would love them all regardless.

On the thought of daughters, Tanta noticed one ahead of her; Kentra Delgoss, outside of her home chopping firewood. The girl that has taken so much pleasure in prodding Tanta's husband, and undoubtedly the reason that Creighton left in a huff those few days ago... Tanta tilts her head forward and marches right toward Kentra. "Kentra!" she calls out as she gets closer. Kentra brings her ax down, cleaving a small log in half, and turns her head to look at Tanta, "Oh. Yes, Tanta?"

Tanta approaches where Kentra is chopping, as she picks up another log and places it on the cutting post. "Would you like to tell me what *exactly* happened the other night between yourself and my husband?" Kentra readies her ax, "I am not sure that it truly matters to you." she replies, as she swings her ax back and brings it down through the log, splitting it with little effort. Tanta is offended by her statement, "It does matter, and in fact it matters quite a lot, Kentra." Kentra reaches down and places another log on the post.

"Why do you not ask him yourself?" Tanta crosses her arms, "Because he left the town, and you know this." Kentra grips her ax in both hands and looks at Tanta, "So he ran away like a puppy from a slap? How surprising." Kentra lifts up her ax, and Tanta quickly kicks the log off the post, Kentra sighs and rests her ax on her shoulder. "Now. What happened?" Tanta says demandingly. "I know it was you, because it for sure was not Hatch or Unet that angered him like that." Kenta puts her left hand on her hip, "Maybe it was Lum, then. If you are going to whittle down the list."

Tanta says nothing, glaring at Kentra. Kentra shakes her head, turns around, and with one hand, plants her ax into the frozen dirt with one swing. She turns back to face Tanta, "I told the Soldier Sir exactly what I think of him, and what I think of how he thinks of other people. I told him that he disgusted me, and that I was not afraid of him. If he did not like it, then he could man up and fight me. That is what I told him, Tanta. But did he? No, he left. He fled. Ran away like a scorned child. Is that how you think the brave, military man that you swooned for should act? Because, myself, I would have expected better of a man from 'Stoen's Legion'."

Tanta gets right up close to Kentra, going chest-to-chest, looking up into Kentra's face. "He left, not because he was scared, but for your sake, girl. Because if he had stayed, he would have made your mother cry with what he did." Kentra does not flinch, in fact she leans into Tanta, "Is that truly what you believe? Because I do not see it that way." Kentra replies. "Of course you do not, as you are too blinded by your own vanity." Tanta is pointing in Kentra's face as she says it. "If Creighton truly wished to, he could kill you before you took one swing of your fist. However he is too much of a gentleman, with too much respect for your father, and for himself, to let you have the satisfaction of allowing you to win by breaking him like that."

Kentra puts her right hand on Tanta's chest and shoves her backward, Tanta stumbles back, falling backward into the snow onto her hands. "I have always known that Creighton was no more than a hound, but I truly thought you were more than just his broken bitch." Suddenly, Tanta sees red, red like the color of her eyes. Tanta quickly stands up, takes one large step, reels her right arm back, and punches Kentra straight in the left eye before she can even react. The impact makes a **smack** so loud that everyone on the street hears it, and despite her massive size, Kentra recoils, almost falling backwards, mostly from shock.

As both of Kentra's hands shoot up to her face to grab her eye, Tanta reaches out with her left hand and grips Kentra by her bottom lip, pulling her forward and forcing them to look eye-to-eye. "Now listen to me, you tree-shaped cretin. I will no longer allow you to disrespect my husband or myself as you have been. Every snide thing you say about him is just as disrespectful to me, and our son, as it is to him, and you are done being so flippant. You are going to cease your mocking, your disrespect, and your active hostility toward any member of the Vordana family. And when Creighton returns to town, you are going to go up to him and apologize for your attitude this last year. Do, you, understand, clearly?"

Kentra says nothing for a moment, her left eye beginning to water, and nods her head slightly. With that, Tanta releases Kentra's lip and steps back, "Now go back to your home, you crass boar!" Tanta screams at her, pointing toward Kentra's house. Kentra quickly slinks away and hurries inside, slamming the door behind her. Tanta takes some deep breaths, and turns her back on the Delgoss home, walking back towards her own.

As Tanta begins walking back toward her home, she feels her heart beginning to slow, and with that, she begins to feel it, the pain in her wrist and hand. That was the first punch that Tanta ever threw in her life at another person. Her whole life, Tanta never had to fight or defend herself, always was quiet and reserved, someone around to take up for her when she really needed it. However, despite the pain in her hand... Tanta felt good.

It was a feeling that Tanta had never experienced before. A rush, an excitement, that was foreign to her. *"If this is what Creighton feels when he fights... no wonder he enjoys it..."* Tanta thinks to herself. She makes it home and reaches for her door handle with her right hand, but winces when she attempts to use the latch. She switches to her left hand and goes inside, where young Creighton II has awoken, and is sitting in front of the fire.

Tanta closes the door, walks inside, and crouches down behind her son, "Did you sleep well, my son?" Creighton II looks up at her and nods, a smile on his face. What a handsome being that her and her love created, together. Tanta starts rubbing her son's back with her left hand, resting her right hand on her knee. *"I will have to go back out and rest this in the snow"* Tanta thinks. However, even with the aching, she feels good. *"I hope Creighton would be proud of me..."*

Chapter #12

[Stoen's Legion]

Creighton Vordana, Joppa Jak, and Brandon Boldwood, along with twenty or so other charge soldiers, are in the back of a covered wagon. They are on their way to a city called Arandro, the last stop before reaching the walls of Lockhart. Joppa is sitting quietly, his eyes closed, cracking the joints in his hands and fingers, deep in thought. Creighton and Brandon are discussing progression and strategy.

"Once we make it into Arandro, we will have sixty charge soldiers take the lead. Before we enter the town, you will take the crate and make the call; if they wish to concede, no blood will be shed." Brandon tells Creighton, who shakes his head, "As much good as it has done so far. Not one of these people has taken the opportunity." "That does not mean that we should not give them the option." Brandon responds, "Aside, for many of these people, their objections are out of fear. They do not know if our word is trustworthy." Creighton rolls his neck, "Because they do not give us the opportunity to show that it is. However, I do not mind. It gives me the chance to stretch my sword arm." Joppa opens his eyes, "Surrender or not, I am simply ready for this exhibition to be complete. I am tired of sleeping in wagons and tents."

Creighton leans out from inside the covering and looks ahead, "I can see the city ahead. Only a short time and we will be at their front gates." Brandon crosses his arms, "Once we establish occupancy in Arandro, the last step on this path is Lockhart, where we will either die or be rewarded. Either way, our journey-" Suddenly, the sound of a bull in agony breaks through the air, followed by screaming from men, and an arrow flies through the cover of the wagon, striking the charge soldier sitting next to Boldwood in the face, "UNDER ATTACK!" yells a man from outside. Brandon, Creighton, and Joppa all stand and bail out of the wagon. Creighton rounds the side of the wagon and places his back to it, followed quickly by Joppa, and the two begin to gain their bearings.

"It seems that they finally internalized that defense was not going to work" Joppa says to Creighton, who has drawn his prime sword, "It would seem so. There are archers in the trees, watch your head." Suddenly, screaming, as men come charging from the woodlands around the road, and closing in the path that the caravan came from. "And we are surrounded" Creighton says, then looks at Joppa, "You cover me and I will cover you." Joppa nods, and the two come out from behind the wagon, Creighton gripping his sword in both hands, Joppa with an arrow nocked.

The charge soldiers have bailed from the inside of their wagons, the ones who had avoided being shot where they sat at least. The first thing that the archers overhead had done was shoot all of the cart-pulling bulls, and they were now aiming for the members of the Legion. Joppa is keeping his eyes up, scanning the treetops, while Creighton takes down any man who charges at the pair. Creighton points to a man in a tree, and Joppa turns, pulls, and releases his short arrow, which strikes the man square in the chest, dropping him from the tree he was perched in.

 A pair of men charge at Creighton, one with a short sword and one with a wood cutting ax. The man with the ax had it raised so far back that the ax head was touching his belt. Creighton with one arm, reposts the sword nearly out of the one man's hands, then push-kicks the man with the ax in the sternum, knocking him down and lodging the head of his own weapon in to his lower back. Creighton turns to the man with the sword and plunges his own sword upwards into the man's chest, coming up out of his shoulder. As he withdraws his sword from the body of his enemy, he looks at the ax wielder on the ground, and before the man can plead, Creighton quickly stabs his sword into his throat and withdraws it again. Creighton observes his surroundings, none of these men are in any kind of proper combat armor.

 In the time that it took Creighton to dispatch those two, Joppa has shot three more men from out of their trees. A man with a knife charges at Joppa, and before Joppa can move, Creighton steps forward and swings the cubed pommel of his sword upwards into the face of the charging man, smashing his nose into pulp. Creighton brings his sword back down at an angle, and plunges the blade down into the man's neck. As the assailant falls to the ground, Joppa nods appreciatively at Creighton. All around them, members of Stoen's Legion are fighting off their attackers. Most of Stoen's charge soldiers are armed with spears and shields, whereas most of these men are wielding small swords, lumber axes, or large kitchen knives.

Over near the front wagon, Brandon Boldwood is dispatching men left and right with his war ax, assisted by half a dozen charge soldiers. Creighton taps Joppa on the shoulder, "Move forward!" The two of them begin moving toward Brandon. A man attempts to ambush the pair from behind the corpse of a bull, but Joppa quickly unleashes an arrow into that man's eye, dropping him instantly. They make it up to Brandon's side, he is now surrounded by dead and dying men, and a few charge soldiers. The majority of the men who came out and attacked them had been dispatched already, by Creighton's count there were less than twenty members of Stoen's Legion in the dirt.

Joppa, Creighton, and Brandon all gather together, Brandon takes a deep breath and calls out "CHARGE SOLDIERS! COME!" All the remaining charge soldiers, over two hundred, assemble in front of their generals. Creighton smirks, "No crate speech for these ones..." The generals follow the charge soldiers and they march into the town of Arandro.

-

The moon has risen on the town of Arandro, and the violence has come to a halt, allowing for the members of Stoen's Legion to take a well-earned rest, including Creighton, who has taken a seat outside the town drinkery, leaning on a barrel of ale, glass cup in his hand, having a hearty drink.

On the ground sat in front of Creighton is one of the charge soldiers, who Creighton has instructed to clean and buff his prime sword, from tip to pommel. Sitting on the bench next to Creighton is Joppa, who has his legs crossed, and is not indulging in the ale at the moment. Around them, charge soldiers, as well as a few other generals, are taking care of the administrative work. Rounding up the citizens who did not wish to, or could not, fight, collecting all of the coin in the city, and so on.

Creighton upends his glass and empties it down his throat, Joppa looks at him "Are you intending to drink that entire barrel tonight?" Creighton wipes his mouth, then dunks his glass back into the contents of the barrel, "I offered to share". Joppa crosses his arms and leans back, "I am not in the mood for strong drink at the moment." Creighton shrugs, and takes another sip, "I must give credit to these people, Joppa. That was the best attempt I have seen so far.

Almost every grown man in this town fought back, it is commendable." "I always respect a man willing to die in battle, even if I am the one causing his end. It is better to die in the field from a fight than of sickness in a bed." Joppa replies.

Creighton raises his glass quickly, sloshing some out, dropping onto the head of the man cleaning his sword, and says "On that, I could not agree more!" Creighton takes a drink. "I am surprised that it took people as long as it has to stop attempting to rely on defense." Joppa leans forward, "In fairness, this entire situation is something that the Lockhart Territory has not seen in, what, four hundred years? Hiding behind walls and attempting to negotiate seems like a good idea. Attempt to calm the situation." Creighton drops his glass into the barrel, empty once again, "But Stoen is not a man to be calmed."

Creighton looks down at the soldier cleaning his sword, "How is my sword looking?" The man looks up at Creighton, "I have gotten all of the blood and dirt off, I still need to buff it, sir." Creighton leans backward and looks up at the sky, "Excellent, good." Joppa clasps his hands together under his chin, "Do you know how many men we lost on our side?" Creighton looks at his friend, "I believe about thirty, most of them outside the actual city." "So what does that leave us with?" Creighton strokes his jaw a little, thinking about how it is about time to shave, before answering "Counting the men who are with Stoen, and Monrow's group, about... one thousand and three hundred, or so. Why do you ask?"

Joppa responds "If we encounter the same kind of civilian resistance in Lockhart that we did here, that may not be enough. Alestin Drow will assuredly have every man under his employ wielding a weapon, plus his normal guard. It worries me." Creighton reaches over and pats Joppa on the back, "My friend, these people out here, they were farmers, hunters, craftsmen. If I know anything about the kinds of people who live in cities, behind walls and surrounded by shops on all sides, they will not have the will to take up arms and fight. Not all of them at least. They will be fully expecting their king to protect them, like a father guarding his child. So I would not worry too deeply."

Joppa looks at his friend, "I suppose you are right. We have done quite well for ourselves so far, once we get into the walls..." Past Creighton, Joppa sees something that troubles him. A man in Stoen Legion attire is pulling a woman by both wrists behind him, she is dragging her heels and struggling quite hard, and a handful of other members of the Legion are ignoring the two. Joppa stands, and starts walking toward the situation. Creighton looks up and asks "What is it?" Joppa puts out his hand, for Creighton to stay seated, "Do not worry yourself. Enjoy your barrel."

Joppa jogs closer to the woman being dragged, and calls out to the man doing the dragging, "Lia, what exactly is going on here?" The man, Lia Benton, stops and the woman looks up at Joppa. Lia is one of the higher ranking generals in Stoen's Legion. Lia looks down at the woman, then up at Joppa "This woman and I are going to go enjoy one anothers company, is all." Joppa looks down at the woman, "She does not seem too keen on the idea." "That is her problem, not mine." Lia quickly retorts. Joppa looks up into Lia's eyes, "This kind of behavior is not befitting of a member of Stoen's Legion." Lia releases the woman's wrists, but looks down and aggressively points at her, a warning to stay put.

Lia tilts his head and puts his hands on his hips, "Well forgive me if I am mistaken, however, you do not appear to resemble King Stoen. Which means that you are not fit to say exactly what I am and am not allowed to do while dawning his crest. So as far as your opinions are concerned, they matter little to me." Joppa looks around, seeing that very little mind is being paid to this confrontation. "Then allow me to speak on my own behalf. I will not stand aside and allow a member of the ranks I serve to lower themselves to such things as you are planning. So unless you wish to have a greater issue with me, personally, then you will allow this woman to go on her way."

Lia shakes his head, then reaches down and snatches the woman on the ground by the collar of her shirt, "I do not care if you do not like me." Before Lia can take a full step away from Joppa, there is suddenly the tip of an arrow pressed to the base of his throat, and Joppa holding the arrow in his hand. Lia looks down at the arrow, then at Joppa's face, "You must not be thinking clearly, General Jak, drawing a weapon on a fellow general." Joppa does not blink, "Let go of the woman." Lia looks around, a few of the charge soldiers under his command come in closer, as well as General Adrick Serint, a bald, muscular man in thick leather armor, and friend of Lia.

 Joppa does not flinch from his position, "What if I told you she deserved it?" Lia asks. "I would not believe you." Joppa replies, when suddenly a hand claps onto his shoulder. It is Creighton, with his knees a bit loose from the drink, followed by a dozen of the men under his and Joppa's command. "Alright, Joppa. What is this?" Joppa keeps his gaze fixated on Lia, "He is attempting to drag that woman away to abuse her." Creighton looks from Joppa to Lia, "Yes?" he asks. Lia looks from Creighton to Joppa and back, "More or less. I think I deserve a little reward for myself, after this bloody day that we have all had."

Creighton nods his head, then looks at Joppa "Is this really a fight you wish to have, my friend?" Joppa quickly and sternly says "Yes." Creighton lets out a sigh and sags his shoulders, "Well alright then." Suddenly he reels back his right arm and punches General Serint in the jaw, knocking him to the ground on-impact. Lia Benton, as well as all the charge soldiers, look at Creighton in surprise. In this time,

Joppa drops his arrow back into his quiver, releases his quiver from his thigh, then tackles Lia to the ground, grabbing him behind both of his knees. Like that, violence breaks out.

The charge soldiers on each side begin throwing fists in accordance with which general is commanding them. Serint quickly mounts his feet again, and he and Creighton grab each other by the collars, and begin exchanging blows. After several punches, Creighton grabs Serint by the back of the head and knees him in the stomach, then drops to one knee, and pulls Serint over his shoulders and slams Serint onto his back. Before Creighton can regain his footing, a charge soldier dives onto him, tackling Creighton to the ground.

Meanwhile, Joppa is kneeling on Lia's chest, raining punches down into his face and head. Lia suddenly reaches up and hooks his thumb inside of Joppa's cheek, grabbing his face from the inside. He drags Joppa down to the ground, and rolls over to mount him. Lia delivers a backhanded slap to the eye of Joppa, and pulls back his arm for a punch, but one of Joppa's charge soldiers grabs his arm. Lia elbows the man in the stomach with the same arm, then quickly grabs his hand and stands up facing the soldier. Lia cranks the man's arm, breaking his wrist, and delivers a stiff elbow to his jaw.

Joppa rolls his weight back onto his shoulders and kicks himself back up onto his feet with one swift motion. He then reaches up under Lia's throat with his arm and grabs him in a choke, quickly squeezing down and applying pressure that makes Lia's face start to turn red. Lia reaches up behind him, grabbing at Joppa's face with his hands, until he finds what he is looking for, and starts to press his right thumb into the eye of Joppa. Joppa leans his head back, but does not release the choke, clenching it harder instead. Before Lia's thumb can make it deep, Joppa is grabbed by the collar from behind, and yanked backwards with the strength of a bull, followed by the ear-rattling sound of a man screaming "ENOUGH!"

It is Brandon Boldwood. Joppa is pulled off of Lia and thrown onto his back, where he clutches at his eye. Brandon grabs Lia by the belt and the neck, lifts him up, and slams him face-down into the dirt. Brandon quickly makes his way through the fighting, forcefully and authoritatively pulling apart each individual scuffle he reaches. Creighton tosses a charge soldier by the head to the ground, and quickly puts up his hands innocently when confronted by Brandon. After only a few moments, the fighting has stopped, and Brandon is standing in the middle of them all.

Before Brandon can begin to speak, he is interrupted by another man "Thank you for breaking up that discourse, General Boldwood..." It is Samuel Stoen, walking up surrounded by well-fitted charge soldiers, as well as Yesha Monrow and a few other generals beside him. "Now, who would like to explain the cause of this ruction between armsmen to me?" Brandon looks around, "You heard the King. Explain!" Joppa stands up, taking his hand from his eye and clasping his fingers behind his back, and faces Samuel "I confronted General Benton, sir. He was participating in behavior that I felt was unbecoming of a man of his ranking, under your crest."

Samuel looks at Joppa, "What behavior would that have been?" Joppa looks down at Lia, who has not stood from where he was slammed, "He was dragging a civilian woman, intending to take her somewhere alone, and use her, without her permission." Samuel looks down at Lia, "Is that so?" Lia grits his teeth, looks back at Joppa, then back to Samuel, and nods. Samuel is silent for a moment, takes a breath, then sighs. "Take them both and seclude them apart." Samuel orders out loud, to nobody in particular.

Two of the generals step from Samuel's side and grab Lia, Yesha Monrow walks over and grabs Joppa by the arm. Creighton steps forward, "Sir, if I may ask, why?" Samuel looks at Creighton and says "I want them held until I can come to a decision, regarding this little skirmish they inspired." Creighton nods his head "I understand. However, then you should know, that myself and General Serint were really the ones who began the violence." Serint, who is laying on the ground, looks up at Creighton, "Hey!" Samuel waves his hand, "Then you two will join them. Men, separate and seclude those four." Brandon yanks Serint up to his feet, Creighton complies with two charge soldiers. The four of them are escorted away, Lia and Serint together, and Creighton and Joppa together.

-

Creighton and Joppa are sitting on the floor of an empty room inside of an old house, a makeshift holding cell of the pair. Creighton has just finished removing all of his armor, leaving him in nothing but his foundational gear. He lies back on the wooden floor, his hands behind his head. Joppa has only removed his boots, but feels completely naked without his bow within sight. Joppa is leaned up against a wall, legs crossed.

"Will he pursue disciplinary action, you think?" Joppa asks Creighton, who turns his head to look at his friend. "Stoen? No, I do not believe so. He does not wish to upset the current rankings given just how close we are to the gates of Lockhart. If I was required to guess, I would say that he will simply wag his finger at us in front of the men and tell us to behave ourselves." Joppa nods, "Us being so close to Lockhart is undoubtedly to our advantage."

Joppa looks at Creighton, "Why did you tell Stoen that you started the fight? Nobody would have told him otherwise, and you would not have been thrown in this cell as well." Creighton shrugs while still lying on his back, "Well for one,

I thought that Stoen would be less inclined to take any serious actions, the more generals that were involved. Also, what kind of example would I be setting for the rest of the men if I let my cohort get reprimanded alone?" Joppa cracks a small smile, "Well it is appreciated, my friend."

Suddenly Creighton's ears perk up. He sits up, looking at the window of their makeshift jail cell, "Do you hear something?" Joppa asks, and then suddenly he can hear it too. The muffled sounds of an extremely heated argument, two deep voices shouting at one-another from inside of a building. Creighton stands up and walks over to the window and opens it up, it sounds like the argument is coming from one or two buildings over, fairly close. Joppa comes and stands next to Creighton to listen. The two of them are not the only ones to have noticed, as several other members of Stoen's Legion are peeking out from windows and doors, or around corners.

One phrase rings out clearly, from the voice of Samuel Stoen, "If you wish to question my integrity, then I will gladly relieve you of your service!", followed quickly by "FINE!" and the sound of a door being kicked off its hinges. From the inside of the building then comes Brandon Boldwood, walking with the conviction of an angry bull. Creighton and Joppa watch as Brandon rips the sleeve from his leather jacket with his bare hand, the one bearing Stoen's crest, and throws it to the dirt. Creighton's eyes widen, Joppa walks away from the window, "Well, it seems that we will not be serving with General Boldwood anymore."

Chapter #13

"The city of Hikline is a truly wonderful, dirty place." Creighton thinks as he walks down the streets. Despite being mostly a farm town, it still has many buildings and shops, along with the Lea of course. The people are bustling around, carting pounds upon pounds of different fruits and vegetables. Two men are pulling a cart by hand that is filled over the brim with hundreds of potatoes. *"That one cart could have fed the entire Legion for a day"* he thinks as they walk by, before arriving at their destination, which is a small open-air shop seemingly run by an old man and a young girl.

After his conversation with Renda yesterday, Creighton has been thinking of what was said, what it could mean, and what he could possibly do. He wants to respect King Stoen's wishes, not spread discontent and concern. However, he cannot help but feel that the threat of a wolf attack becomes more real with every detail that is uncovered about the situation. Creighton looks around, and sees a small store with the sign "The Scratched Helmet", an armory shop. That may not be a bad idea at all, some new protection for himself. After what happened to his armor from the Legion... a story that Creighton regrets to recall.

Creighton walks over to The Scratched Helmet and walks in through the open door. As he enters there is a man sitting in a chair reading a book. Judging by his leather chestplate and the shortsword on his hip, he is likely the guard. Barely paying attention to what is going on around him, he does not even look up as Creighton enters. Creighton looks down at him, seeing that the man's sword is on the outside of his belt. He could snatch the man's sword from him in a second, if he wanted. Inside this shop is a certain stink in the air. The stink of smoke, but not from a forge or a fireplace, from pipes.

Over near the counter there are two older looking men, one on the customer side and one on the shop side. They both have pipes, the one on the shop side, presumably the owner of the place, has a wooden one with a huge bowl about the size of Creighton's palm. The smoke in the air is thick enough to sting the eyes and make it hard to see clearly across the room. The owner and the older man are speaking about different kinds of metals, when he suddenly notices that he has a prospective customer.

"Aye! Hello there, stranger. What are you looking for today?" the owner calls out to Creighton, who looks around the room. "I was thinking about picking up a new piece of armor for myself, maybe a friend of mine. Nothing particular in mind." The owner slaps the counter in front of him, smoke swirling around his hand as he does. "Well we have only the finest and most combat ready wares, here! I am sure you will find something that strikes your taste."

Creighton walks over to a table with different chest plates laid out. Most of them seem very flat, not having the curve that you would suspect or imagine a piece of armor like that to have. Quite uncomfortable for sure. Creighton picks one up in his hand and examines it closely. It feels thin, and soft, like even a stone from a sling would break through.

"Ah, you like that one?!" the owner calls out, "That is a fine piece of steel, is it not?" Creighton turns around with the plate in hand, "If I were you, I would not brag about a piece like this. Flat as a dinner plate and I think I could put my fist through this if I was determined enough." The owner stands up on his toes to get a better look at what Creighton is holding, "Ah, I see. That one was made by my brother! He is new to this, and a bit of a fool. I will have a talk with him." Creighton tosses the lousy piece of armor back onto the table, clanging as it hits.

Creighton continues to browse the shop, he can hear the owner and his smoking friend chatting, "I do not know who would ever bother to carry a poniard on their person. A knife like that, I would rather carry around a stick with a brick tied to it." says the friend, "Ey. A real man just carries a proper sword, or at least something respectable like a baselard. That is a knife with some muscle to it." Creighton cannot help but to roll his eyes at the mere premise of the conversation. Clearly neither of those men had ever been in any sort of true combat.

After a moment, Creighton sees something that catches his eye all of the sudden, a very fine looking helmet that is a near replica of the one he was given with his old suit from the Legion. A nice, dark grey steel in the sallet style. The visor is also the face guard, with a gross cut out of the center of it to allow for both unobstructed sight and breathing, and the whole thing can be pulled to the top of the head if you need to expose your face. Creighton walks up to it and places his hand on the top, turning it to inspect the sides as well. The owner sees him taking an interest in that one and walks over to him.

"A lovely helmet right there, that is." he says as smoke billows from his mouth, "Forged that myself by hand, inspired by the great and honorable King Stoen himself! His men always have such dazzling armor, would you agree?" Creighton picks up the helmet in both hands, "Yes, they always have. This one reminds..." he stops speaking as he begins to really get a feel of this helmet. Creighton puts the heels of his hands on the edges of the neck of the helmet and begins to press. With very low effort, the metal helmet begins to bend. The owner sees this and snatches the hemet from Creighton, "What are you doing?! Do you have no respect for the property of others?"

Creighton points at the helmet, "If I can bend that thing that easily, I doubt it would stand up to any kind of combat." The owner sets the helmet on the floor behind the counter,

"Well, I will have a talk with my brother about his smithing skills, then." Creighton crosses his arms, "You just said you forged that yourself." The owner waves the comment off, "It is hard sometimes to remember sometimes which ones are his and which ones are mine." "So each piece of armor that is shoddy or lousy, is made by your brother, is what you are telling me?" the owner nods, "It seems so." "Is your brother here right now? I might like to talk with him about his creations." The owner leans back on the counter, huge smoking pipe in hand, "He, um, is... out of town at the moment. I do not know when he will be back, either."

The owner puffs on his pipe, not looking at Creighton, "Do you have no pride in your product? I would not trust a single thing in this entire shop to keep me safe in a battle." The owner looks at Creighton with a lour expression, "I am quite happy with my steel, thank you, sir. I have not received many complaints, either." Creighton leans on the counter, "It is difficult to complain when you are dead." The owner puts his pipe in the corner of his mouth, "Once they take it out of my shop, what happens to them is none of my concern." "How many men do you think have been killed or wounded while bearing your shoddy armor?" "I do not care."

As a man who has spent much of his life at arms, that answer rubs Creighton a very wrong way. Creighton grabs the pipe from the man and pitches it across the room, the owner steps back with an appalled look on his face, "You are perfectly content with men out there dying because of your garbage?" The owner points at Creighton, "You can leave." Creighton shakes his head, "Answer me." The owner waves the guard by the door over, who through all this, has yet to stand up, "Clem! Come take this git out of my store!"

Creighton continues to stare a hole through the owner, who appears both annoyed and scared. "Since you wish to disrespect me, you will be leaving now." "It is only 'disrespect' if you were deserving of respect in the first place." The owner gasps and places his hand on his chest. Creighton hears the guard approach, and he reaches his hand out to grab Creighton's shoulder, "It is time for you to-" before he can touch him, Creighton snatches the guard's wrist, yanking him forward while also kicking the guard's leg out from under him.

Clem, the guard, is yanked down and his face is smashed into the edge of the counter, busting his lip wide open, splattering blood on the counter. Before Clem can even react to what has happened, Creighton reaches down, pulls the guard's sword from his scabbard, and takes a step back. The owner does not move, the guard crumples to the ground holding his face, and the smoking buddy has his back to the wall watching this all happen, eyes wide and still puffing his pipe. Creighton opens his mouth to say something, but is interrupted, "Be done playing wit' your new friends, Creighton!"

All the men in the store, except the guard, look toward the door. There stands Renda, tucking the owner's pipe into the inside of her vest. "T'ere is someone you want to talk to at my drinkery. Come." Creighton looks back at the owner, points at him and says "Take some pride in your work." then turns around and walks to the door, still carrying the guard's weapon.

Creighton and Renda walk outside, Creighton begins to inspect his new sword. A decent edge to it, a bit scratched up, and the tip is not too pointed. It will make for a great blunted trainer. "So, I am guessing you were not happy wit' his products?" Renda asks, "Not just that he sells shoddy armor, but also that he does not care that it is. If he had made my armor from the Legion, I likely would not be here." "Mah! Youda been fine! It is hard to kill a man like you." Creighton lays the sword on his shoulder, "Who am I going to speak to exactly?" Renda looks up at Creighton, "Trust me, he will be able to help enlighten you about the whole... wolf situation."

As they are walking, suddenly the door to a small bakers shop bursts open. Two men from the King's Army come out dragging a young man and throw him face-down to the ground. They are easy to identify as the King's men, given their adorning of the color green and the crest of the king on the forearms of their armor. All of their attire that is not steel is dyed the color green, the same dark green that King Stoen is so fond of, the most prominent part of it being their boots. One of the king's men places his foot on the back of the man, while the other begins tying his hands. Creighton and Renda quickly walk around the situation, "Hm, I wonder what that is all about." Renda immediately replies, "Ah, he got caught with a stack of the King's Parchment." Creighton looks down at her, "How would you know that already?" Renda puts her hand to the side of her mouth and whispers, "Who do you t'ink helped him get it? *Hehehe*"

-

Creighton and Renda get back to the Q, "So, where is this man I am to speak with?" Renda points to the corner of the room. There sits a man donned in the armor of the king's army, with two upturned mugs and another in his hand, leaning back in his chair. "He has had some drinks t'at just so happened to be a *bit* stronger t'an normal. He came to help knab t'at boy wit' t'e parc'ment, and I have a feeling that he might have some t'ings to s'are if you, if you ask nicely." Creighton claps Renda on the shoulder, "He and I will have a chat…" he says with a smile.

The Q is fairly busy given the time of day, loud and bustling with life, and paying customers. Creighton walks through and past drink tenders and customers until he gets to the table he is looking for. The drunken man does not notice

Creighton approaching until he has already set a chair down next to him, "Hello there, friend." he says with some difficulty. Creighton smiles and nods, "Friend is correct. You serve King Stoen, correct?" The drunken army man nods exaggeratedly, "Well I served with him in his Legion." The man leans forward "Wow, truly? That must have been quite the adventure! To actually fight alongside the man himself! Watching as he took cities single handed and put this whole territory over his knee." Creighton nods, unsure of how to take that assessment of Stoen, "It was indeed. I was hoping that you and I could have a conversation, one man at arms to another." Creighton rests his hand on the man's shoulder.

Chapter #14

The sun has risen once again on The Q, but Creighton has already gotten himself dressed and prepared to head back to his home. Last night he had commissioned Renda to give his traveling clothes a nice rinse and scrubbing. While the dirt has been cleaned off, he cannot help but notice a certain must still coming from them. Hopefully she did not just "clean" them in her bathwater. He exits The Q after giving Renda a wave goodbye, moving quickly as he has a cart to catch that will be passing through Stonewater. Creighton had given the Cattle-Master fifty coin to allow him to ride on the back until they reached his home. Creighton gets to the wagon, greets the man, and hops on the back, dropping his things next to him. The Cattle-Master and his young daughter are loading bags of potatoes and onions into the wagon while Creighton gets comfortable.

He got very little sleep last night, spending hours speaking with that man from Stoen's army, and buying him a few more drinks to keep his lips loose. Most of the conversation was not quite as fruitful as he had hoped. However, there was one useful thing that Creighton was able to get from the man, and that is why people are being arrested for speaking about the wolf attacks. It is not so much the discussing of the attacks, but rather the implying that there is more to it than just the wolves. The man said that people who claim it is more than just wolves are "inciting fear" and "attempting to spread discontent". Essentially, King Stoen does not want people thinking, or knowing, that these are not just the acts of wild animals, but rather targeted attacks at members of the legion.

Creighton intends to sleep through a large part of this trip. The bull begins to pull the cart, the Cattle-Master and his daughter up at the front. The shaking and light bouncing of the cart begins to lull Creighton into slumber, and dreams enter his weary mind.

In his dream, Creighton finds himself wandering through a forest, the grass is tall and wet, the leaves overhead are dense, allowing very little light to shine through. He walks through the knee-high grass, his pants and boots getting more soaked with each step taken. After some time, the faint sounds of a whining puppy ring through the forest. He continues to walk, slowly and cautiously through the woods, until he spots a clearing. In the clearing, there is a small wolf pup, still of suckling age, laying next to a large, dead eagle.

Creighton approaches it, prods the pup in the side with his boot, and the pup turns to snap at Creighton with his tiny jaws. Creighton looks around the clearing, there are no other wolves around at all. This pup must be alone, Creighton surmises as he reaches to grab his sword, to put the pup down. Something as young as he would not be able to survive without his mother. However, at this point, he realizes that his sword is missing.

As he notices this, a bear suddenly comes from the dense grass like a fish breaching the waters. Creighton quickly backs away from the pup and the bird, and the bear pays him to mind. The huge beast slowly approaches the pup, who turns and bears his teeth, while whimpering in fear. The bear lifts his arm and slaps the wolf pup away, sending him skittering away. The bear picks up the eagle in its mouth, crunching it down between his mighty jaws, and swallowing its body hole.

Witnessing this, the wolf whimpers, before letting out an air-shaking howl. Creighton covers his ears and ducks his head, and the bear recoils as well. After a long time, the howl ends. Creighton releases his ears and looks up, and suddenly, the wolf pup has grown to be twice the size of the bear. He slowly begins to approach the bear, who roars at the giant wolf. The wolf responds by lashing out, and biting down on the head of the bear, and lifts him into the air. The wolf begins flailing the bear around like a hare, until the rest of the body tears from the neck, sending the lifeless body flying into the dense grass.

The wolf spits the bear's head onto the ground, then looks behind him at Creighton, his mouth now covered in blood. The wolf and Creighton lock eyes, and the wolf howls loudly again. Suddenly, a pack of wolves rush up from behind

Creighton. Two jump and grab onto each arm, one by the wrist and the other by the elbow. Creighton tries to shake them off, when two more come from behind and rip bloody chunks from his calves, causing him to fall to his knees with a scream.

He is being held in place on his knees by the wolves. The giant wolf slowly approaches Creighton, its giant paws sinking into the dirt, too heavy for the very earth itself. In a blink, the giant wolf suddenly lurches his jaws forward and bites into the head of Creighton.

Creighton wakes with such a jolt that he falls from the cart, hitting the dirt path and looking around frantically. There is nothing but trees and rocks, and the cart stops, "Are you hurt sir?" the Cattle-Master's daughter yells. Creighton blinks and rubs his head, "No, I just fell. My apologies." he replies, standing back to his feet. Creighton walks back over to the cart and jumps back on. "Continue." he says to the two, and with that, the Cattle-Master smacks the bull and they continue on their way. "We will be stopping in Jethro for the night, and continue on our way as soon as the sun rises in the morning." Creighton nods his head, not speaking. He is still thinking of that dream he had, what it was all about... likely nothing. Horrors caused by a lack of rest, that is all.

-

Almost three days, down many dirt and stoned roads, through a dozen settlements and towns, and finally Creighton and the wagon he is riding on are approaching Stonewater. During their stop in Maulin, Creighton used the last of his prize money that he had kept to buy Tanta a new headband that he knew she would like. As well as some smoked meat for himself to finish off the trip. The bull pulling the cart slows to a stop, and Creighton hops off the back with his things. He gives the Cattle-Master a polite nod, as he and his daughter walk around the back to begin unloading the cart.

Creighton walks into town, the sun is setting, and Creighton is happy to be home, poison having been purged from his veins. He passes by the communal wood storage, and he hears a call from behind him, "Creighton!" yells a woman's voice Creighton turns around to face her, and it is Kentra. She had just dropped a bundle of wood, and the flesh around her left eye is dark. She walks up to Creighton, her arms crossed. "I, would like to apologize for my words, and attitude last time we spoke. I was, out of line, and it was... inappropriate." She says while staring at Creighton's chest. Creighton smiles, reaches out and slaps the girl on the shoulder, "Accepted. You have a fine night, Kentra."

Creighton walks away, and Kentra stomps her foot and walks back to the wood storage, her pride slightly wounded. Creighton gets to his front door and opens it, casually strolling inside. Tanta is sitting by the fire reading, Creighton II is asleep. Tanta stands "Ah, welcome my love, I am surprised that you have returned this soon." Creighton walks over and gives his wife a quick embrace and a kiss, "I took care of my poison, and returned to you as soon as I could. How are you and the boy?" Tanta looks over to the bed of their son, "We are well. You were only gone a short while, so little has changed."

Creighton walks over to his and Tanta's bed and begins to disrobe, "One thing has, Kentra has realized her place." Tanta smirks, and sits back down in her seat behind Creighton. "Is that so?" "Yes. She caught me and apologized for her actions from before I left. Her eye was dark, so I suppose that Hatch beat some manners into her." Tanta smiles and turns her head, "Yes, I would suppose so." She stokes the fire a little, deciding to not mention the truth about Kentra.

Tanta cannot help but to look at the brand new boots that Creighton left at the end of the bed, however she does not comment. It is not worth the words nor the chance. Creighton remembers, "I bought you something." He walks over to his bag, after rummaging through for a moment, he finds the headband that he bought, inside of a small wooden box. He stands and hands it to Tanta, "I saw this on my journey, and thought you may like it." Tanta takes the box, it is not often that Creighton buys her a gift like this. She opens it to reveal the headband, she pulls it out to feel it. The hairband is silk, smooth and shiny, and dyed a bright, rose red, Tanta's favorite color. Across it is stitched a shallow flower pattern, the thread being the same color as the silk.

Tanta looks up at Creighton, "It is beautiful. Thank you, my love." She gives him a kiss, then walks over to her drawers and sets it down, "I will wear it tomorrow. My old band was starting to stretch out, anyhow." Creighton sits on the edge of his bed and runs his fingers through his hair, it had been a long trip. Tanta turns around, and sees a new sword. This one, she must ask about. "Did you purchase that blade on your trip as well?" Creighton looks at Tanta a little confused, then remembers, "No, I won it, actually." Tanta tilts her head, "From… the Lea?"

Creighton shakes his head, "No, in a... duel with a man from the city. I defeated him, and he gave me his sword." Tanta squints her eyes at him, "Alright, he did not give me his sword, but I still took it." Tanta lets out a small chuckle, "Some habits are forever, it seems." Creighton reaches over and picks up the blade, "I needed a replacement anyhow, for the one I gifted Gesa. Looking at the craftsmanship of this sword, it is only fit for blunting anyhow." He gives it a one-handed swing at the air, "You could barely cut a cat with such a thing."

Tanta looks to their sleeping son, who has not moved during this whole conversation, "Maybe you could gift that one to young Creighton. I am sure he will need his own training sword, correct?" Creighton nods, "Yes, however, I already know which of my blunted swords I will give him. I have known since the day he was born." Creighton sets down the sword, "And I hope that when he gets it, he wields it well." Tanta walks over and sits next to her husband, "With you as his teacher, I am sure he will make an exemplary swordsman."

Chapter #15

Dozens of carts are being pulled down a large dirt road, surrounded on all sides by hundreds of men-at-arms. Creighton is sitting in the back of the front-most cart, alongside Joppa Jak, and Samuel Stoen himself. Creighton is using a whetstone to smooth out the edge of his knife, as he had already shaved his sword down to the finest edge that he could get with a simple handheld stone. He used his knife for cutting threads and prying nails more than he had for fighting, but that was no reason to let it be dull. You can never know when your prime weapon will be struck from your hands.

Joppa is sitting cross-legged, fiddling with one of his arrows. He inspected all of them before the caravan began its journey, so he is confident in his weaponry. Samuel is sitting at the front of the covered part of the wagon, writing in a journal, as he often did. A simple recounting of the events that transpired through this whole expedition, from his perspective, of course. Joppa can no longer hold his tongue, and feels the need to ask. "King Stoen" he says out loud, and after a few seconds Samuel responds, "What is it?" Joppa slips his arrow back into its quiver, "If I may ask, what happened between yourself and General Boldwood?"

"First off…" Samuel claps his journal closed, "He is no longer a general, so do not refer to him as such. Secondly, it does not matter, that business is between he and I." Joppa nods, "Understood. I just could not help but be curious, as everyone in the town heard the commotion from your argument. I was not sure if it was something that we should be concerned about." Samuel sets his journal down, "He wished to question my integrity, my honor. He disrespected me, and for that he was stripped of his place in this legion. Boldwood is a bullheaded idealist, and now I no longer wish to speak of him. Yes?" Joppa nods.

"And what of Lia?" Creighton chimes in. Samuel looks to Creighton, "What of him?" he asks. Creighton inspects the edge of his knife, "After what happened in Arandro, I am a little surprised to see him still leading his troop." Samuel leans back in his seat, "It was just a hot-blooded skirmish between men. Nothing to flog or strip rank over." "With complete and utter respect, King Stoen, that is not quite the part I was referring to." Creighton retorts. Samuel looks at him, then to Joppa. "Lia is a fine man, he was just lacking judgement that night. He has been reprimanded, I assure you." Joppa crosses his arms, "I do not trust the man." "Well if you're lucky he'll catch an arrow to the chest while we raid Lockhart." Samuel snaps back.

He stands from his seat, "Listen to me, both of you. Do not make any more issues with Lia, or any of your fellow generals, understand? Within the next few days, none of you will ever have to see the others again. And the last thing I need is discourse among my ranks, potentially ruining my day of triumph. So you, Vordana, Benton, Monrow, and all the others *will* work together like brothers on a farm. I do not care if you like or hate one another. Do you understand?"

Joppa nods his head, Creighton nods and sheaths his knife. "Very well." Samuel Stoen sits back in his seat, "Soon that inert fool, Drow, will be off the throne, and in the ground. I will be in his place, and the territory will be better for it, especially the likes of you, my loyal generals. The Lockhart Territory will be stronger, more fierce, and more prosperous. We have for too long been weak, while places like the Markall and Pestian territories grow stronger by the decade. We, Lockhart, are the center of the territories, and yet Alestin Drow has made us feeble, something to be pushed around. Not respected. It sickens me."

Creighton nods his head, listening to his King's words. It is true that Lockhart has become more lax, for lack of a better word, over the last four hundred years, as that was the last time Lockhart had experienced any kind of widespread conflict. However, Creighton still does not remember hearing any derision from people of other territories. When he lived in Markall, Creighton only heard positive things about Lockhart. Joppa looks to Stoen, "Is that the inspiration for this rebellion? To restore respect to the territory?" Stoen nods, "Yes. That is why you are here, and that is why I must take the territory from Drow."

"And here I thought it was because Drow spanked you in public and kicked you out of his army" Creighton thought to himself, a thought that he would never dare speak aloud. While he would never speak it, his sentiment held some truth. Stoen is a former member of King Drow's military, holding a fairly high rank, before being publicly ousted for insubordination. The exact story and reasoning is highly debated, but one thing is known for sure, and that is that Samuel Stoen's grudge was strong. Creighton assumed during this whole escapade that this was all for revenge, however Samuel sounded genuine in his words just now. Maybe Creighton had misjudged his leader... or maybe Samuel is a talented liar.

Joppa responds to Samuel's previous comment, "A noble pursuit, I'm sure that is why you have amassed this great following, that marches all around us. Aside from the mercenaries like myself and Creighton, of course." Samuel nods, "Yes, we are surrounded by great, bright minded men. Men who know a good cause when confronted with it. Their spirits are why we will take Lockhart with relative ease. I am confident in it." *"Bright minds are quite the stretch..."* Creighton thinks. "A strong spirit is the greatest advantage in any conflict," Joppa replies, "We are truly fortunate to be backed by such men."

Their conversation is interrupted by the voice man at the front of the caravan, General Hagar Mancrusher. "LOCKHART IN SIGHT!" he shouts out with his deep voice. Samuel Stoen stands from his seat, "Well, it appears that the time is truly almost upon us, my men. What do you say we hop off, and join Mancrusher at the front?" Joppa and Creighton both nod, and hop off the back of the wagon, moving around the sides so as to not impede the wagon behind them, followed quickly by Samuel.

The caravan is moving at a slow, steady pace, so it is not hard for the three men to quickly make it to the front. Up at the front is Hagar Mancrusher, a proud man with a barrel chest, thick arms, and long, flowing golden-brown hair. Over his shoulder, he holds a war hammer, with a head the side of a toddler. "Hello my King" he says, as Samuel and the other two join him. "We should be at the gates of Lockhart before the sun starts to set." Samuel looks toward the city on the horizon, "Excellent. It has been a long two years, but it will be worth it once his head lays upon the street."

-

The sun is on the horizon as they approach the front gate of Lockhart. The caravan is not received warmly, however. The gate is closed tight, and they can see the top of the wall are dozens of archers, ready to draw if given command. Stoen calls for the caravan to come to a halt about one furlong from the front gate, and gestures to the three generals standing around him, as well as a pair of Shield Carriers. The six men walk closer to the gate, Samuel in the center, and the Shield Carriers in the front.

At the top of the gate, stands King Alestin Drow, and by his side, his Great Auxiliary, Mallnue Youngstead. They close enough distance where Samuel Stoen feels that his voice will be heard clearly, "Good evening, Drow!" he calls out. For a moment Drow does not respond, then "I will not partake in badinage with you, Stoen. Nor do I wish to battle." Stoen shakes his head, "Neither of these things are your decision to make, Drow. That is why I come to you with a verbal gift. The opportunity to surrender. If you open the gates and submit yourself to me, no other blood will be spilled. Not of your army, nor your people, nor your Auxiliary!" The Great Auxiliary steps forward, as if to speak back, but is stopped when Drow places his hand upon Mallnue's shoulder.

Hagar Mancrusher, standing between Creighton and Joppa, leans to Creighton and asks "Is the Great Auxiliary wearing a blue helmet? That is quite strange." Joppa answers instead, "That is no helmet, Hagar. It is the man's strange, defining feature." and he is correct in saying this. Beyond his place by the king's side as Great Auxiliary, Mallnue

Youngstead is known for one thing, and that is the brilliant blue hair atop his head. Most people assume that he inks it, that it is some kind of odd aesthetic choice, however there is rumor that it sprouts from his scalp that very color.

King Drow calls back down to Stoen, "I have no intent of letting you into my city, or of simply allowing myself to be executed. You were once a well respected member of my ranks, and now you have brought it to this. It is quite disappointing, however I am unsure if I should place that burden on you, or myself. If you attempt a siege, you will not access the inside of these walls, and you and your paid army will be killed. Those who are not killed in the attempt will be executed for treason. So I plead with you, Stoen. Turn around, and go."

Stoen shakes his head, "We both know it is far too late for that, Drow." With that, King Drow turns and walks away, followed by Mallnue Youngstead. After a moment, all the archers along the wall pull up their bows and nock arrows, but do not pull back their strings. "I believe that is a hint" Hagar says, Stoen nods "I agree. Raise your shields, and let us return to the caravan." The Shield Carriers raise their shields, the three generals and Stoen huddle behind their protection, and they walk back to the caravan.

-

Back at the caravan, they have set up a small camp. A large portion of the men have been set up on watch, however, the odds of men coming out of Lockhart to attack are quite low. Around a campfire sit Creighton, Joppa, Yesha Monrow, and Hagar Mancrusher, the only one of them partaking in strong drink being Hagar. Creighton sharpened his blades during the trip, so he is simply staring into the fire, thinking of his plans for tomorrow. Joppa is enjoying a fresh plate of fire-roasted mushrooms, while assembling new arrows with a few of the men under his command, not just for himself, but for the rest of the Legion's archers as well.

Yesha is speaking with Hagar, recounting stories of valour while he uses his spear to roast a goat steak, "-and so the cows were running around like mad, my general was swinging in the wind, and I could not even find my boots!" says Hagar, causing he and Yesha to erupt in laughter. Hagar takes a swig of his tankard, then says "After that, I decided that the Mildrea Territory was not quite to my liking, and came back home." Yesha claps Hagar on the shoulder, "Nor mine, my friend." Yesha looks over at Joppa, "Have you been outside the territory, General Jak?" Joppa responds while fastening an arrowhead to a shaft, "I spent much of my youth in the Pestian Territory, it was quite the experience. However, I do have family up toward the north, that I may go visit if we survive tomorrow."

Hagar pulls his cup from his mouth, "Bah! I have few doubts that we will survive. It has been over four hundred years since there has been a war in these parts. None of the men in that city's *grandfathers* have ever seen active conflict! They will not know what hit them." Creighton, who has been sitting silently, nods his head, "True. That might just be why Stoen looked for outsiders, like us, to make up his ranks." Joppa finishes his last arrow, and hands it to one of the men who was helping him, "That would make a lot of sense. In addition, I have seen Stoen reading historical books on the art of warfare. He is no fool, for sure."

Hagar looks around the campfire, all the generals have their respective weapons by their sides. "Speaking of fools, let me ask you fools a question. How did you choose your weaponry?" Hagar reaches down to his side and lifts his maul-style war hammer up by the neck, an unwieldy thing that few people have seen him actually swing to great effect. "Like me, back when I was promoted from a lowly spear-bearing charge soldier, I decided that I wanted something with a little more... Power." With the last word, he slams his hammer into the ground, kicking up some dust. "My uncle taught me how to fight with a hammer, in fact! And after only a few weeks, he taught me everything I needed to know. What about you all?"

Hagar lifts his hammer and points at Creighton with the head, "You. What made you decide to pick up the two-hand sword?" Creighton pulls out his sword, a fine piece of steel that any warrior would be happy to hold. "Back where I come from, a sword is actually the second weapon you are taught to wield. I mastered the spear faster than any of the others in my group, so I was quickly introduced to the sword as well. This specific one, I have had since. This is not the one that I was issued though, I had it commissioned." Creighton flourishes his sword, allowing the light of the campfire to shine off of the polished blade. "And it is still beautiful."

Hagar drops his empty cup, "Too shiny for my tastes!" Creighton rolls his eyes a bit, and Hagar stands from the log on-which he sat, "I must go and relieve myself" he says as he walks away. Yesha tosses another stick in the fire, checking how his goat is cooking, Creighton looks at him, "What made you decide to stick with the spear?" He asks, as Yesha's weapon of choice is indeed a spear, despite him being many years past that of a charge soldier. Yesha smiles and shrugs, "There is nothing wrong with a good spear, is there? Has the reach, it is versatile, you can throw it if you need, and I have trained with it since before I was a man. Do not misunderstand, I have tried other weapons. Swords, axes, bows, flails, hatches, nothing else really ever felt quite right in my hands."

"That is why I love my bow." Joppa interjects. "It feels comfortable, and I have been training with it since the age of five." Creighton raises his eyebrows, "You were shooting arrows when I was still tackling my brothers around the chest." he says with a small chuckle, Joppa nods, "And that is how perfection is acquired. Hours, days, weeks, years of practice and repetition. That is why I can shoot a robin out of a tree from a hundred paces." "Quite the boast!" calls out Hagar Mancrusher, as he is returning to the fire, "However, can your bow back up your words?"

Joppa stands from his seat, picking up his bow. "I would be more than glad to show you." Joppa takes one of his arrows and points to a dead tree outside of the bounds of their camp, "Take that tankard of yours, and hang it on one of the branches of that tree, over there." Hagar picks up the metal cup, shrugs, and walks over to that said tree, about one hundred and ten paces away, and hangs it on one of the lower hanging branches. And not three seconds after his hand was no longer touching the cup, it was suddenly pierced with an arrow with a sharp *clang!*

Hagar jumps back in shock, as he hears some of the men, including Creighton and Yesha, laughing at his surprise. The tankard rocks on the branch, the short arrow stuck through the side, having almost gone clear through. Back at the fire, Yesha turns his steak and says "You may have made the poor man soil himself, Joppa. He jumped like a hare." Joppa sits back down, and Hagar returns to the campfire, shot-cup in hand, "Well, it appears you tell no lies, General Jak!" Joppa smirks, resting his bow by his side. "Now, if you will excuse me, I must find a new cup..." Hagar sets the tankard with the arrow in it on the ground, and walks away.

The other three generals collect themselves, Yesha pulling his finally cooked steak off his spear. "What are your plans, after all is said and done in the Legion?" Yesha asks Creighton and Joppa, "Myself, I am going to settle down I think. Buy a nice piece of land and spend the rest of my years hunting and fishing." Creighton sits back and thinks for a moment, "Stoen offered me a piece of land anywhere in the territory. I will claim it, and other than that, I am not sure." "Maybe find a woman, make a couple kids?" Yesha asks. Creighton shakes his head, "I do not think so. I still have my youth and my strength, I doubt I will settle for quite some time."

Chapter #16

Tanta is walking down a rocky road, a large satchel slung onto her back. She's returning home from a town up the road called Reede, a town about the size of Stonewater, but with more farm work. Creighton had agreed to watch their son for a little while so she could take this little walking trip. It was a little over an hour's walk each way, but Tanta does not mind it at all, in fact she enjoys it. This day trip has been the longest amount of time that she spent away from Creighton II since birthing him.

As much as she loves her son, sometimes it is nice to have some alone time. Besides, Creighton should be able to take care of his son as well, and Tanta has faith that he can manage it for half a day, at least. As she walks, Tanta begins rooting through her bag. The entire point of this trip after all, aside from time alone, was to get herself something sweet. There is a baker in Reede who made little treats that he called "Bee Berries".

They are small berries that are covered in hardened honey, and it was Tanta's favorite treat, even if they did hurt her teeth a little bit. She pulls one out of the bag that she bought and begins to suck on it, softening the outer shell. The last time that she had these was half way through her pregnancy, where Creighton had paid Joppa to go up to Reede and get her a large bag of them. It was all she ate for two days, and it apparently was the entire batch that the baker had made that day. This time she bought only a modest bag.

Tanta is excited to share these with her son, as Creighton does not enjoy honey. While Reede is much closer to Stonewater than it is to Lockhart, Tanta knew of Bee Berries long before ever moving to her current home. On her travels in her younger days, with her parents, she had been to Reede several times, and every time she made sure to get herself a nice bag of them.

Her parents had moved far from the Lockhart territory around the time that Tanta had been recruited to be one of the King's cooks. They had never met Creighton, something that she hoped to change, one day. Now that Tanta was thinking about it, Creighton had never mentioned his own parentage… it made her wonder if it was just something that slipped his mind, or if there was a good reason for it. Either way, Tanta thinks that she may ask him about it when she gets home.

As Tanta is taking in her surroundings, swimming in her own mind, and happily snacking away on her treats, she realizes that she has almost made it back to Stonewater. As she nears the town, she stops, and sighs. She stands in place for a moment, taking in the quiet of the woodlands, and looks up into the blue, cloudless sky. After a few moments, she bites another bee berry, and continues toward Stonewater.

Stonewater is bustling, everyone going about their daily work. The tanner is tanning, Gesa is helping his mother clean vegetables, Lum and Kentra are splitting logs. As she walks by, she gives Gesa a small wave, which he returns. She can see that he has the training sword that Creighton gifted him on his belt. Tanta had left for Reede just as the sun was beginning to shine, so it was a little after mid-day now that she has returned. Tanta opens the front door of her home, unaware if anyone is inside.

As Tanta walks in, she sees that both her husband and son are sitting inside at the table. Creighton immediately stands from his seat, and Tanta drops her bee berries in horror. "It is not as bad as it seems." Creighton reassures her... but does not de-escalate her shock. "What happened?!" she screams at her husband. Creighton II, her son, currently has his entire head haphazardly wrapped in bloody bandages, and dried blood all down the left side of his face. Tanta quickly sets down her bag and runs over to his son, inspecting the bandages.

Creighton steps back, crosses his arms, and looks to the ground. "Well, we were out hunting, and after a while we did not find anything worth shooting. He got weary, and started pitching rocks at the squirrels in the trees. One of them hit a branch, bounced back at him, and..." Tanta looks up at Creighton, "Why were you letting him throw rocks at squirrels?" "He was having fun." Tanta shakes her head, "How long ago did this happen?" Creighton looks out the window, "I would say, maybe half an hour. I got him back and bandaged the split in his face as soon as I could, but I have never been one for stitching."

Tanta points over to where they keep their medical supplies, Creighton quickly retrieves it for her. In the bag are many things, including a needle and special wound sealing thread. This was not to be the first time that Tanta stitched a wound closed, but it was the first for her son. "Now, my son, I am going to pull off the bandages and get you cleaned up. It may hurt, but mother is going to make you better." she says to Creighton II. He takes a sharp breath through his nose and nods.

Tanta begins slowly stripping off the bandages. While Creighton did not wrap it very cleanly or tightly, he did do a good job of packing the wound to help stop the bleeding. As she pulls off the last of the bandages, she sees the cut. It is almost the length of her index finger, but not too deep. Tanta dumps some helda, a wound cleaning solution, onto a small cloth, and presses it against the cut. Creighton II flinches and cringes a bit, but does not whine or cry. Creighton steps closer and places her hand on Tanta's shoulder, "He did not cry a single tear, from the time the stone split his face, to the time I packed the wound."

Doing her best to be gentle, Tanta cleans the wound and all around it. With her touching and moving of it, it begins to bleed a little once again, but only a little. Tanta quickly threads the needle, and presses it against the edge of the cut, "Be strong, my son, this will only sting a little." Tanta pushes the needle up and through the cut, and the boy barely whinces. Tanta continues to stitch the wound, one stitch at a time, closing up the split in his head. Creighton remains silent, standing behind his wife as she does her work.

After several minutes, Tanta has fully closed the cut across her son's head, who is breathing heavily, but did not whine or squirm at all during the whole process. Creighton is filled with pride, and Tanta is filled with relief, now that the wound is closed. Creighton hands her a warm, damp rag, that he retrieved while she was finishing up, to clean their son's face. Tanta cups Creighton II's cheek in one hand, and begins to wipe away the mixture of fresh and dried blood from his face. He squirms more during this than he did during the stitching.

Creighton smiles, and places his hand on his son's shoulder, "You took that well, my boy. I am proud of you, you are as tough as your father!" Creighton II smiles, and looks up at him. Now that she can see that he is fine, Tanta has fully calmed down. "Well, now that we have that taken care of," she shoots her husband a quick, annoyed glance, "I brought you something, my son." Tanta walks back over to the satchel that she tossed to the ground and picks it up. She places it on the table, and pulls out the bag of honey treats that she had bought, "Hold out your hand. These are some of my favorites. Try them."

 Creighton II holds out his hand, and Tanta drops a few of the hardened honey treats into his palm. He takes one in his fingers, and places it in his mouth, crunching it between his teeth. His face lights up, enjoying this new flavor, and quickly tosses the handful into his mouth. Tanta laughs, and reaches back into the bag, "I know you do not like honey, so I got you this." Tanta pulls out a fresh, huge bread roll from the bag, wrapped in a thin cloth. It was bigger than Creighton's fist, and was coated in butter. While it had long since gone cold, it was baked fresh this morning, and still nice and soft.

 He accepts the roll from his wife, and thanks her with a kiss. Creighton II stands from his seat and pulls on his mother's sleeve, she looks down at him, and he holds out his hand for more bee berries. Tanta gives him a few more, "That is the last of them for now. We do not want to eat them all at once, they can last for a few days, if we are responsible." Creighton II tosses all the ones he was given in his mouth again, then nods.

"Now, you need to be careful until that cut fully heals. You cannot be playing too rough, or climbing on things," she looks at her husband again, "or throwing rocks, until it is

ready for the stitches to come out. Do you understand?"
Creighton II nods, then walks over to the front door, and
outside. "If he comes back bleeding again, it was not my
fault." Creighton says, in jest. Tanta shakes her head, and
playfully pushes him away from her.

Chapter #17

[Stoen's Legion]

The sun has not yet risen, but the men of Stoen's Legion have begun to move, readying themselves for assault. Creighton and Joppa are together, surrounded by the men under their command. The job of their battalion is simple; break down the front gate. It is a large, wooden gate, as wide as ten average men, and as tall as five. They have been given oil and torches to try and light the gate ablaze, weakening it for penetration. It was likely well treated wood, so that would not be the end solution, but they have plenty of tools to work with, and about fifty men under their command to accomplish this goal.

Hagar Mancrusher will be nearby them, he and his men are on the ladder charge. Simply enough, they are the ones running at the wall with ladders to try and climb over the walls. Yesha is in charge of protecting and escorting King Stoen, and Generals Benton and Serint are on their own separate assignments.

Right now, they are all standing at attention, waiting for the go-ahead. Creighton is both a little nervous and a little excited, this is the first time that he has ever assaulted a castle. Joppa is showing no signs of any kind of nerves, however. Creighton looks down at his friend, who is kneeling in the dirt, hands in his lap, taking slow, deep breaths. "You seem exceptionally calm, Joppa. Is this not your first time?" Without opening his eyes, Joppa responds, "It is not my first, nor my second. I have learned that one must be clear headed in order to have success at such things as these. If you let the 'excitement' get to you, and lose focus, that is how you make mistakes, how you get caught from the side or behind."

As Joppa says this, one of the charge soldiers kneels down next to him, laying his spear by his side, and placing his hands in his lap. Joppa looks at him from the side of his eye, but does not comment. Creighton rolls his shoulders, "This is my first wall assault. It is nothing I am not confident that I can do, just a new experience." Joppa releases a breath, "Everything in life starts as a new experience." Creighton looks ahead, he can see dozens of men aligned at the top of the wall, likely armed with bows. As Creighton begins to think, he suddenly feels the light of the sun kissing his neck, and then…

BBBRRRRR! The sound of a horn being blown shakes the air, and men start screaming, running toward the walls of Lockhart. Joppa Jak hops to his feet with one swift motion of his body, pulling his bow off his shoulder. he and Creighton share a look, then Creighton calls out "Charge!" to their men. As their name indicates, the charge soldiers ready their spears and shields and charge toward the gates of the city. Creighton is at the front of them all, followed by Joppa, and flanked on their sides are four shield bearers, two on each side.

Far off their side, they see Hagar Mancrusher and his battalion running with their ladders. Hagar is lagging behind, but not by choice. Once Creighton and Joppa's battalion approaches, Joppa stops and holds back a bit, along with a dozen other archers, and two of the shield bearers. Joppa and the archers begin firing at the defenders on the wall. As the defenders attempt to shoot back, it quickly becomes obvious why Stoen chose this exact time to launch the attack; the rising sun is leaving the defenders nearly blind. A dozen more archers come from someone else's battalion to join Joppa.

While Joppa and his men are providing covering fire, Creighton and his men approach the gate, the charge soldiers have their shields raised above their heads to block arrows and rocks, the shield bearers are covering Creighton. He calls to one of the Commanders in the battalion, ordering him to douse the gate in oil. Rocks and arrows are raining down on the men at the gate, one arrow slipping past the shields and going down through the foot of one of the charge soldiers, who screams and drops his shield.

Creighton snatches him by the collar and pulls the soldier under the protection of the shield bearer that is protecting him. The commander and three other charge soldiers carry two large pots full of oil over to the gates. The others do their best to provide overhead cover, as they set one pot at the base of the gate, and use the other to douse the wood of the gate the best that they can. More rocks and arrows come down, a few soldiers get knocked down or hit, before they finish dousing. They toss the empty pot aside, and Creighton calls out to retreat. He grabs the man who got shot in the foot up under the arm, "Limp fast", as the battalion retreats toward the line of archers.

All of Creighton's men make it a safe distance from the wall, except for one man, who dropped his shield to a rock and took an arrow through the eye. Joppa readies his bow, and an arrow keeper ties a pitch-covered cloth to the tip, and lights it with a piece of flint and steel. Joppa draws back, quickly takes aim, and releases the burning arrow. It flies down range, and strikes the side of the full pot, igniting the oil that was inside and causing a modest fireball that caught on the oil that they had thrown on the gate, causing the whole thing to light ablaze.

While it was quite the spectacle, it will take a bit of time for it to burn the gate, and even longer before they can safely run back up to it. At the top of the gate, men quickly start hauling pails of water up, to try and dump it on the fire. Joppa and his men begin to specifically target anyone who appears to be holding a bucket or pot. Creighton stands back, briefing his men on what will be done next.

While they are going about their business, Hagar and his ladders are not doing so well. As quickly as they are being put up, they are being pushed back down. So far two men have been injured from being hit with falling ladders, and one has had his head split open with a rock. Hagar gets frustrated, and puts up a ladder, using his arms and body to brace it up, to keep them from pushing it over from the top. Surprisingly, it does work! But, as soon as his men get to the top, they are knocked off the side, one dying before impact, and the second dying on impact.

Hagar sends up a shield bearer first this time, to cover for the rest. The man climbs up trying to keep the heavy shield above his head with one arm. He gets to the top, and one of the defenders attempts to push him off, but the shield bearer is able to push forward, and actually make it to the top of the wall! The shield bearer pushes a pair of defenders back one way, when another comes to stab him in the back, only to be stopped by one of Hagar's men.

But, before more men can make it up the ladder, two defenders manage to get behind the three men who made it to the top, and both use their full bodyweight to shove the ladder backwards, one of the defenders going too far and accidentally propelling himself over the edge, falling head-first to the dirt below. Hagar cannot support the weight of the ladder, as well as two men who were in the process of climbing it at the time, as it tips back, and is forced to move out of the way, allowing the ladder, and men on it, to hit the ground with great impact. The one higher up is wounded gravely, and the lower one was able to bail before impact, breaking his ankle but otherwise being alright.

Hagar punches the ground in frustration, and screams "Damn you, just let it happen!" at the wall. At the top of the wall, the men who made it up are doing their best to defend themselves, and causing an effective, chaotic distraction, allowing for less archer fire from the defending side and drawing a useful amount of attention. The fire on the gate is already beginning to dim, the oil having burned away fairly quickly, leaving just the wood to burn. Joppa has done a fine job of keeping the defenders from dousing it, although the fact that it is an oil fire, buckets of water likely would not have helped them much.

Hagar continues to try and climb the walls with his ladders, Joppa and his men exchange arrows with the defenders atop the wall, and Creighton is ready in wait, waiting for the gate to have stopped burning enough to charge it again. Himself, as well as several other charge soldiers, are armed with large, heavy axes, fit for chopping down trees. Hagar gets a few more men up the wall, but they do not manage to last long, before being pushed off or overwhelmed, while still taking a few defenders with them.

Creighton has decided that the time has come, and calls at his men to follow him, and they charge back at the wall. Shield bearers in the front and on the sides, covering them from arrow fire, but there are much fewer than there was the first time. Joppa himself has hit over twenty men. Creighton and his fellow charge soldiers begin hacking away at the wood of the gate. The lumber is thick and strong, but the burning has helped to weaken it a fair bit.

The blackened wood comes off easily, breaking and chipping away. But once they get to the white wood underneath, it immediately becomes harder. The axes stick more, and less comes away. As Creighton digs his ax into the gate, he hears screaming coming from behind, and something hot splash against his calves. He turns around to see that three men had just had boiling water dumped onto them from above, one was holding a shield above his head, the other two were not so lucky. *"That is much worse than rocks"* Creighton thinks, "If you are not chopping, shields up!" he calls to his men, "Cover anyone who cannot cover themselves!"

The shield bearers are already providing cover, and the rest of the men cover themselves with their shields as well. Another pot of boiled water comes down, splashing off mens shields, or off the ground. The splash is still hot and still hurts, but it is nowhere as bad as taking the brunt of it to the neck. There are fifteen men chopping away at the gate, trying to get through with all their strength. Suddenly, one man takes an arrow through the calf from the side. He falls backward, bumping into a shield bearer, right as another pot of boiled water is dropped onto them, scorching him, the bearer, and another man, who fall to the ground in pain.

It is at this point that Creighton is beginning to worry; they are barely making a dent into the gate, they are being bombarded from above, and a lot of men are getting hurt. Before Creighton can come to a decision, he hears the sounds of conflict and distress coming from overhead. Suddenly, two of the defenders fall from the top of the wall, hitting the ground hard, and the sounds of panicked battle. Creighton comes out away from the gate, looking up at the top of the wall, *"Did Hagar actually make it up?"* he thinks to himself.

At the top of the wall is not Hagar, but rather General Benton, who drives his hatchet into the neck of one of the defenders, and tosses him over the inside edge of the wall. Surrounding Lia are nine charge soldiers, each bearing either a sword or a spear, and they are working their way toward the center of the gate, where the mechanism to open the gate is located. *"How did he get up there..."* Creighton wonders. All the archers have ceased fire, and Joppa has jogged up to Creighton's side, alongside his men. As Lia and his men clear their way to the mechanism, Lia stops and leans over the edge of the wall.

"Thank you for the distraction, boys! And you are welcome." The gate begins to ease open, "The wonders that you can do with a couple of climbing spikes, eh?!" With that, Lia pushes off the edge and continues to make his way down the length of the wall, taking out any who hold a weapon and do not bear the Stoen crest. Joppa nods, "We were but a diversion... how nice for us to know that." Joppa pulls and nocks an arrow, and charges through the gate, followed by his men.

Creighton follows him immediately, jogging into the city, dropping the wood ax that he had, and having his sword at the ready. Having already lost track of Joppa, Creighton gets his bearings, looking around his surroundings. After a few seconds, he realizes that the only men at arms around are his own. Except for a few corpses that fell off the wall, there are no defenders to be seen, no resistance or defense are at the ready. Creighton walks down the main street, looking left and right. No ambush, no battalions at the ready, nothing.

He looks ahead, toward the entrance to the Black Castle, the main keep of Lockhart, and not even a line of defense there, Creighton feels that something about this whole situation is just... wrong. Before he can get too much deeper into his contemplations, he gets a stiff, metal hand clapped on his shoulder, the hand of Samuel Stoen. "This, this is fine work, General. Would you not agree? One of the simplest wall breachings that will go down in the history books. Now come, bring your men and follow me. We have a castle to impregnate."

Samuel Stoen walks forward, flanked by Yesha Monrow, and the most heavily-armed of all the Charge Soldiers, and all of the highest ranked Commanders in the army. Creighton follows, when suddenly the group is split apart and run through. There are two men carrying Lia Benton up under his arms, who has an arrow sticking out of his back, poking through his chest. Everyone allows them to pass, but nobody comments out loud, *"Lia must have encountered some resistance on the wall, I suppose"* Creighton thinks, before refocusing himself, and following the prospective King Stoen to the front gates of the castle.

Chapter #18

Creighton and Gesa Het are down by the river, walking along the rocky shore of the riverbed, both of them holding a blunted sword in their hand, and neither of them are wearing boots. Gesa is grunting through it, the rocks digging into his soles, while Creighton seems unphased. "Sir Vordana, why are we doing this again?" Gesa asks, "You have learned to hold and swing the sword with some proficiency, which is good. However, your footwork is lacking, and that can be more detrimental to you in a fight. It does not matter if you have the sword of a god and the arm of a giant, if you trip over yourself and fall to your back."

Creighton stops and turns to face Gesa, "Alright, stop." Gesa stops, grimacing, and adjusting his footing, trying to find a more comfortable position. "We are going to go through some of our regular drills. This time, focusing on footwork. Now take your stance." Creighton takes his, readying his sword. Gesa slowly gets into his stance, having to adjust his feet several times in a few seconds to find something comfortable.

"I will agress first. Ready?" Gesa takes a deep breath, then nods. Creighton quickly steps in and lunges his sword forward, a two-handed stab at Gesa. Gesa is unable to move, takes the rounded tip of the sword right into his chest, and falls onto his rear end. "You did not even attempt to dodge or parry." Creighton steps back, and Gesa stands back up, "It hurts to move my feet." Creighton rests his sword on his shoulder, "More so than that strike to your chest?" Gesa touches his chest, "No, I suppose that hurts more..." "Exactly." Creighton retorts.

"Your turn to come at me." he says to Gesa, as he takes his stance again. Gesa takes a few quick breaths, then brings his sword up above his head for a downward strike. As he steps in to deliver the blow, a pain moves up his leg, causing him to lose focus and commitment in the swing. Creighton easily parries the swing, grabs Gesa by the collar, and lightly strikes him in the stomach with the pommel of his sword. "Do not fall", Creighton says, as he then shoves Gesa backwards. Gesa stumbles back, keeping his footing with a bit of struggle, but does not fall. "You are in control of your body, boy. Make it work for you, make it work through the pain. Some uneven, sharp-edged rocks are nothing. Now, prepare to defend."

Gesa nods, pats himself on the face, and shakes out his ankles. Creighton paces back and forth for a moment, before coming at Gesa with an upward strike toward his side. Gesa is able to bring his sword down and block the strike with the flat of his sword, one hand on the hilt and the other open palm against the inside flat, absorbing the full impact with a loud clack of steel. Creighton retreats,

"Excellent block, Gesa. But do not forget about follow ups. When the attack has been foiled is the best time to strike your opponent, be it with a block, parry or dodge." "Yes sir." he responds.

Creighton invites Gesa to attack him with a wave of his hand. Gesa grips his sword and attempts a lunging stab, like Creighton had done to him. This time, he is able to keep his footing true, through some discomfort. Creighton slips to Gesa's right side, avoiding the stab, and using one hand to slap the flat of his blade into Gesa's calf. Gesa gasps in pain at the hit, and turns to face Creighton, having learned long ago to not let Creighton have his back during training. A good way to catch a stiff slap to the back of the head. "Not bad, good form. Now, this next one, I want you to avoid. Do not block or parry it. Whatever way you want to move is up to you."

"I will." replies Gesa. Creighton grips his sword in one hand, up against the crossguard. He pulls his arm back and swings horizontally at Gesa's neck, but the boy ducks and quickly steps backward, keeping in form. Creighton notices that Gesa's rear leg buckles a little bit from a particularly rough rock, however he keeps his composure. "Excellent dodge, Gesa. And the rocks seem to not be bothering you as much as before?" Gesa shakes his head, "No, sir. I just try to ignore it." Creighton smiles, "As long as it works. What we will do now is some of our basic drills. However, once again, you are to focus more on your footwork than normal."

Creighton walks up and faces Gesa, "You start with the 1-2-3." The 1-2-3 is a simple drill, the one on offense tries an overhead strike, then a side strike, then another overhead from the opposite side, the one on defense just blocks them all. Gesa takes his turn on offense, Creighton blocks all three with little effort. Creighton takes his turn, and Gesa blocks all three, but it takes much more effort on his part. As Gesa takes his turn on offense, Creighton asks "So how are things with Lum?" Gesa finishes his turn and pulls back his sword, "Well, things are goin-OW!" His words are interrupted by Creighton smacking him on the shoulder with his sword, "That was not an invitation to stop the drill, talk and block." Gesa shakes off the smack, and blocks the last two attacks while responding, "They are good! She is great."

Gesa takes his turn on offense, "I have gotten much closer with her parents as well." Creighton takes offense, "What does her sister think of you?" Gesa misses the last block slightly, Creighton's sword knicks his elbow. Gesa sucks air through his teeth, but does not complain, and takes offense, "Kentra is... her and I get along fine. What about you two?" Gesa almost manages to strike on the second swing, but Creighton blocks all three, then takes offense. "Her and I are on better terms, ever since Hatch had that 'talk' with her." Gesa takes his turn on offense, "Right, I remember that, but...” Gesa swings too wide on the last one, missing Creighton entirely. Creighton responds by stepping in and shouldering Gesa in the chest, knocking him backwards, but not to the ground.

Creighton nods approvingly, “You took that well. However-” before Creighton can finish his sentence, Gesa responds “There is never an excuse to miss your opponent, yes I remember. Sorry, sir.” Creighton sticks his sword into a space in the rocks, “Apologize to yourself, not me.” Creighton turns around, stretching his arms over his head. “Let us take a break. The river is good for sore muscles, give that a try if your feet are aching. Gesa tosses his sword and starts walking toward the water, “Ah-ah-ah!” Creighton calls out, stopping Gesa in his tracks, “Do not just toss that thing aside like a pig bone. Pick it back up and put it down with respect.” Gesa walks back over to his sword, picks it up, and wedges the tip down in the rocks, like Creighton did with his.

“There, now you may rest.” Gesa walks over, hikes up his pants, and lowers his legs into the cool, rushing waters. The strength of the water gives a bit of moving pressure, like a massage, and he breathes a sigh of relief. “So were you saying something before? I feel like your statement was unfinished.” Creighton asks, as he also rests his feet into the river. Gesa takes a moment to consider, he does not know if it is his place to mention that it was not Hatch that had a "talk" with Kentra. "There was not, I was just saying how I remembered that." Creighton rolls his neck, "It is a miracle what a stern strike can do to fix a disrespectful mouth. Especially that of your child."

Creighton looks to Gesa, "Do you intend to put a child into Lum, Gesa?" Gesa turns bright red instantly, "It was a question, not a pot of boiled water, my boy." Creighton laughs as he says. Gesa, flustered, replies "I, we, have not quite thought that far." Creighton shakes his head, "Come, now. Two young and growing adults such as yourselves, I cannot imagine such things have not come up. Especially at night, when you two are alone, beneath a blanket on a cold night."

Gesa tucks his head down, staring at the waters, "Fine, you do not wish to discuss such affairs. To each his own. When I was your age, back where I come from, I was familiar with many ladies, local and visiting. Truth be told I cannot be entirely sure that young Creighton II is my first child." Gesa looks up, "Really?" Creighton nods, "Yes. I was a strapping young man, not quite as chiseled as I am now. However, I wore a military uniform, and that certainly helped down at the inns and drinkeries."

Gesa dips his hands into the water and splashes it on his face, "I do not think military life would suit me well." He says with a tinge of sorrow, Creighton simply shrugs, "It is a hard life, not fit for all. However, if it brings you a measure of comfort, I can say that, as you are right now, you would make a better soldier than many I have seen." Gesa leans back on the rocks, "Is that so?" "Yes. I have seen some quite terrible soldiers in my day. Served alongside and fought against. It is quite the sad thing, really. Seeing someone spend so much time, effort and dedication, only to be struck down in their first battle. It feels like a waste of a life."

"That would be quite the shame, I imagine." Gesa replies. Creighton is quiet for a moment, "It is. On the other hand though, I have had the honor of serving alongside some truly accomplished veterans as well. Men who spent their entire adulthood on the battlefield, or carrying a weapon as their profession. Myself, I am happy with the time I spent, but I am also happy with when I decided to get out."

Gesa turns his head to look at Creighton, "Because you met Tanta?" Creighton nods, "Yes, indeed. She changed my whole life. If not for her, I may still be living in Lockhart, serving King Stoen. Or going around doing mercenary work. But, with her and the boy... I am glad that I retired as I did."

"Where do you think your life will be in twenty years?" Gesa asks. "Twenty? That is quite a time..." Creighton takes a moment to think, "I would like to think that Tanta and I will still be here, maybe with another child to our legacy. And Creighton II is working under the Stoen regime. Possibly as a knight, or a castle guardian." "He certainly is growing large, I am sure Stoen would love to have a giant in armor bearing his crest." Gesa replies, and Creighton is taken aback, "A giant… my son…"

"My love!" calls out a woman's voice, Creighton turns around, to see it is Tanta, with Creighton II by her side. He has grown quite a lot, standing just taller than his mothers elbow. "Yes, Tanta?" He calls back to her, "You have a man who wishes to speak with you, back at home." Creighton is surprised, he was not expecting a visitor. He stands up, and looks down at Gesa, "It seems I have business to tend to. Do some more movement drills before you go home." Gesa nods, "Thank you for your time, Sir Vordana." Creighton walks over, pulls on his boots, and jogs over to Tanta. "Did this man give his name?" Tanta shakes her head, "He said he is an old friend of yours, from the Legion." That definitely gets Creighton's attention, as the only man that he considers a "friend from the Legion" at this time, is Joppa, and Tanta would recognize him, obviously. "Let us go."

Creighton takes the lead ahead of Tanta, who has young Creighton II by the hand, leading him behind at a brisk pace. The three of them return to Stonewater, and begin walking back towards their home. As they get closer, Creighton recognizes the man who has come to visit. He is on a bench outside of Creighton's home, but stands as the three approach, "General Vordana! It has been quite a time…" he says jovially, but with a tinge of nervousness. It is Lia Benton.

Chapter #19

Lia and Creighton are inside his home, Creighton has asked Tanta to stay outside for the moment. Lia is sitting at the table, fingers laced and leaning on the edge with his elbows, Creighton is standing over him, his arms crossed over his chest, looking at the man he once served by. Little has changed, save a few wrinkles across his face, except for one thing; a long horizontal scar across the center of his forehead, from one side of his hairline to the other. Crieghton recognizes it well, it's the mark of the Crimson Mask. The Crimson Mask is a great mark of shame for anyone who considers themselves a warrior. It means that an enemy defeated you, had you fully at their mercy, and instead of deciding to kill you, they deeply cut your head open to let the world know that you were not only bested, but are only alive because your enemy did not deem you worthy of even killing.

And now Lia bares it, a scar he did not have during his time in Stoen's Legion. "We have not had a conversation since the Legion was disbanded, and now you show up to my home, expecting to be addressed like an old friend. What are you doing here, Lia?" Creighton asks, deciding to not ask about the scar. Lia rubs his mouth with his hand, then sighs, "You received a letter from King Stoen, correct? About the wolves?

Creighton looks over his shoulder, to ensure that the front door is closed, then nods. "Well, recently there was another attack. Do you remember General Inaer?" Creighton shakes his head, "The name sounds vaguely familiar, but no." "He was killed in his woodland home. His family was torn asunder by wolves, and his head cleaved from his shoulders. It made me think… I have a son now, Creighton. I could not bear the idea of him being turned to wolf shit because of me."

"So you have fled to my town, to put *my* son in danger?" Creighton asks with indignance. Lia stands from his chair, "You are already here, are you not? As far as I remember, the two of us held the same rank in the same army. Aside, those first letters came in, what, three or four years ago? Seeing as you are still in the same town that you moved to when Stoen relieved us all, you do not intend to leave any time soon, anyhow. My thought was this; if I stay here, it does not increase the chance of an attack on this town, but it negates the chance of an attack on the town of my son and his mother. I have come to you, to ask for your blessing, and I thought that if someone does come with a pack of wolves, two of us would stand a better chance of fighting back than one. If you truly feel my presence here is unwelcome, or a threat, then just say so."

Creighton caresses his chin, thinking on Lia's words. He speaks no lies, as far as Creighton can tell, especially regarding better chances if they worked together. Lia is far from a man that he considers a "friend", however, he does not harbor the same ill-will that Joppa did. Creighton nods his head, "Alright. You have my blessing to seek refuge in Stonewater. However, do not think you will be bunking in my home, but I will help you find work and shelter." Lia nods in acknowledgement, "That was all I asked for. Thank you, Vordana." Creighton looks to Lia again, and decides to ask.

"I must ask, General Benton, what is the story behind…" Creighton taps his forehead, to which Lia gets a look on his face as if he had just bitten into sour meat, and looks to the floor. At this moment, there is a knock at the door. Creighton decides to not push the question further, "Come in" he calls out. Tanta pushes the door open, young Creighton II by her side. "Is everything alright?" she asks. Creighton gives Lia a quick look, then back at Tanta, "Yes, all is well. General Benton is going to be moving into town." Tanta smiles, "Well I am happy to have you here. Any friend of my husband is a friend to me, as well." "I am glad to hear that, thank you for your goodwill." Lia replies.

Creighton points to the door, "Go wait outside, and I will come get you in a moment." Lia nods, then walks toward the front door, Tanta and the boy moving out of his way. As Lia gets outside, Creighton says "Close it." Tanta does so, and young Creighton II walks over to his bed and starts playing with some toys he has. Creighton leans against their table, sitting on the edge, "General Benton. As in Lia Benton?" Creighton nods, "The very same." Tanta looks back at the door, then to Creighton "Correct me if I am wrong, but I do not remember you or Joppa ever speaking *highly* of General Benton." she says in a hushed voice.

Creighton strokes his chin again, "We did not. However, Joppa was the one with the personal vendetta against him. Myself, I have no strong feelings. I am quite surprised that he is all the way down here. To my knowledge, he was still living in Lockhart. And I doubt that those walls would be easily breached by wolves..." Tanta sits on the edge of the table right next to Creighton, "Well, it has been quite some time since you last saw each other. It is not unreasonable to think that he moved." Creighton nods, "That is true."

Tanta places her hand on top of Creighton's "It has been years, and we have not yet fallen victim to one of these wolf raids, let us hope that it never comes. But if it does, you will keep us safe, and with the help of Lia, I am sure that there is nothing to fear." Creighton grabs Tanta's hand, "Your confidence is appreciated." he pushes himself off the table, "Well, I suppose I should help him get settled in." Creighton gives Tanta a kiss, then walks out the front door.

Creighton exits the house, Lia is in the street, looking around at the town, "This is a lovely little town, Creighton. How many people are here?" "About fifty, depending on the time of year." Creighton responds. Lia puts his hands on his hips, "Out of the way, away from the crowds and noise of places like Lockhart." Creighton walks up next to Lia, "My thoughts, exactly. Now come, I have an idea for what you can do." Creighton and Lia begin walking down the road.

"Remind me, Joppa moved here as well, did he not? Is he still around?" Creighton shakes his head, "Not for a few years now." Lia kisses his teeth, "Likely for the best, he would not have been as welcoming. Where did he get off to, do you know?" "He just said he was going north, he did not inform me of what town." That is not true, however. Joppa did indeed tell him the town he was going to, Starlight, but Creighton did not feel that that was information that Lia needed to know. "Well, I hope he is well."

As they are walking, they see Kentra and Lum working together to carry a large crate of wheat seed for their family's storage. Creighton waves at them, "Delgoss girls!" he calls out. The two women stop and look at them, "Yes, Creighton?" Kentra asks. As he and Lia approach them, Creighton gestures at Lia, "This is one of my old associates, General Lia Benton. He is looking for work and lodging. I believe that your father may be able to help with both, if I have heard correctly." Lum looks at her sister and nods her head, they both set the crate down, Kentra rolls her shoulders. "Well, we have a spare room, and my father has been wanting help tending to the cows, since Kentra and I have been spending so much time helping Adin down the road. Do you know how to take care of cows, Lia?"

Lia shrugs, hooking his thumbs on his belt, "I am familiar with the smelly bastards." Lum nods her head, "Good enough. Come, I will introduce you to my father." Lia walks over and follows Lum as she walks toward the door to her home, Kentra watches her go and throws up her hands, but does not say anything. Creighton points to the crate, "Would you like help with that?" Kentra thinks for a moment, then waves him over, "Sure, if you please." Creighton walks over and grabs one of the rope handles of the chest, as does Kentra. They both lift it together, Creighton grunting, but not straining too hard. Still, this was a testament to the natural strength of the Delgoss family.

They begin carrying the crate toward the entrance to the Delgoss cellar, not too far from where it had been set down. Once they get to the doors, they set the crate back down, and Kentra fishes the keys from her pants. Creighton flicks his wrists, "Quite heavy." "Yes." Kentra replies, as she unlocks the cellar and opens both doors. They both pick the crate up and slowly haul it down the stairs, Creighton being the one to walk backwards. The cellar ceiling barely gives room for Creighton's head, his hair brushing against the untreated boards that hold the dirt in place above their heads.

They set the crate of seed down in a corner, next to two other containers, one of corn and another of wheat. They also have some meat hanging, drying out. "Thank you," Kentra tells Creighton, who gives her a small pat on the shoulder, "Glad to help. If you are in need of any other assistance, just let me know." With that, Creighton walks up and out of the cellar. As he reenters the sunlight, Hatch is walking out of his home with his arm around Lia's shoulders, "-and that would not be the first time! But anyhow, let me show you the cows. We have some for meat and some for milk." Creighton can see Lia clenching his fists, but going along with the large, muscular man.

"My father was happy to accept the help." Lum says to Creighton, who he had not noticed. "However, your friend seems, irritable." "He is not quite my friend. As I said, just an old associate." Lum shrugs, "Whatever he is, seems grumpy. And speaking of your associates, how is Gesa doing with his sword?" Creighton turns and smirks, "I could ask you the same." That gets a hearty laugh from Lum, then Creighton answers her question, "He is doing well. The boy has come a long way, gotten proficient. Still has a long way to go, however."

Lum has composed herself, and crosses her arms over her chest, "That is good to hear. He does practice quite a bit when you are not around. I am not any sort of judge on swordsman quality, but he seems more comfortable swinging around that piece of steel that you gave him, at the least." Creighton nods, "Makes me happy to hear that." It fills Creighton with great pride to see how Gesa has come along, ever since that first day out in the woods.

While his father is little in the way of a role model, Creighton has been able to help the boy gain some confidence, as well as teaching him a skill that he will be able to use for the rest of his life. It gives Creighton faith that maybe this whole fatherhood thing will be manageable. "Sir Vordana!" he hears someone call out, that someone being Gesa. Gesa is still bootless, carrying both of their swords from the riverbank, "You left your practice sword by the river." Creighton and Lum share a look, then Lum locks eyes with Gesa. Gesa sees Lum glaring at him, and drops the practice swords. Lum takes off in a dead sprint toward her lover, who responds by turning tail and running away. Creighton just shakes his head.

Chapter #20

Stoen leads his men toward the front gate of the Black Castle, the heart of Lockhart. By his side and around him, in addition to almost one hundred charge soldiers, are his most trusted generals; Yesha Monrow, Joppa Jak, and of course Creighton Vordana. They approach the gate, Joppa and the other archers look to the windows, but there are no archers to be seen. As they approach the front gate, Stoen calls out "Bring the bulls!"

Hagar comes up, leading a pair of large, muscular bulls. Affixed to the bulls is a huge, metal and wooden contraption that looks like a giant wedge. They stop them a fair distance from the gate, Stoen and the others move out of the way, giving the bulls a clear path forward. One of the commanders cracks a whip at them, and the two bulls charge forward, quickly gaining speed. The bulls reach the gates, and *Bam!*, ram into the middle of the two gates, causing them to crack, but not burst open yet.

Consternation and panic can be heard from inside, Creighton can hear it. However, there it is not as loud as he would have expected. The commander in charge of the bulls escorts the bulls back to where they started. He reaches under the giant wedge contraption and gives both of the bulls some kind of treat, before walking back behind, and cracking the whip again. The bulls charge forward again, and this time as they strike the gate, they plow straight through, knocking both doors of the gate wide open, and throwing back a few men who had been standing on the inside of them.

Creighton and the rest of the generals charge in, surrounded by their men. Inside there are three men who had been knocked down or out by the bulls entrance, and two dozen men waiting at arms. One thrusts his spear at Creighton, who parries it down, and stomps the weapon out of the man's hand. Before Creighton can advance on the defender, three charge soldiers mob him, cutting him down in seconds. The rest of the defenders fare about the same, only two members of Stoen's Legion taking a meaningful wound, as the defenders are overwhelmed in power and numbers.

Stoen comes in behind all of them, "Generals Vordana and Jak, take your men and go clear the east wing! General Mancrusher, you do the same to the west. Monrow, you stay with me. Remember, those who lay down arms, allow them to live. Any others, treat them like the rest." he says as he gestures to the corpses of the defenders on the floor. All the generals bow their heads, and signal to their men to follow. Samuel Stoen and Yesha take their brigade of eighty men and walk down the main hall of the castle, toward the throne room.

Creighton and Joppa lead their men down the west wing of the castle, Joppa asks Creighton under his breath, "Why are there so few men defending a king's castle?" "The same thought had crossed my mind..." Creighton replies, as they lead their men down the wing. Creighton and Joppa take turns kicking open and checking each and every room that they pass. Most of them are empty, or have a few of the castle servants hiding. With each group of cowering servants, a pair of charge soldiers are instructed to take them and escort them out of the castle.

After clearing a few rooms, and finding no resistance, they approach a fork on the road. One is the kitchens, and the other is a flight of stairs going down into the depths of the castle. "I will go down, you clear the kitchen. We will meet outside afterwards." Joppa says. Creighton nods, and Joppa takes fifteen of the men and heads downstairs. Creighton now has about twenty men left with him. They approach the doors of the kitchen and attempt to push them open, but they are being held closed by three defenders.

Two charge soldiers ram their shoulders into the door, but it barely budges. As they throw themselves against it again, Creighton grabs the metal body shield from one of the Shield Bearers, and signals his two burliest men to follow him. Creighton put his arms in the handles of the shield, and the two burly men grab and put their shoulders against the edges of it. "On three. One... two... Three!" The three of them charge forward, slamming with all their combined might into the center of the two doors. With that amount of dispersed power, the doors are knocked open, throwing two defenders back, and one stumbling back away without being struck.

The two who were knocked down immediately get back to their feet and pull their weapons, Creighton takes the large shield he is holding and smashes the one in the face, knocking him down and out, while the other is cut down by the two burly men who helped Creighton with the door. Creighton tosses down the shield, and sees that the third defender is on his knees, sword in front of him, and his hands raised above his head. The young defender has a look of pure fear across his face, Creighton points at him and says "Smartest one so far."

Looking around the room, as Creighton's men come in around him, immediately taking the surrendered defender and dragging him out of the room, Creighton sees that there are no more armored defenders, but back in the corner, attempting to hide behind crates of grain and fruit, are a couple of castle servants. He calls out "No one over there has a weapon, do they?" There is a prolonged silence, before Creighton gestures over toward them, signaling his men to go get them. Five men walk over there, toss the small crates aside, and start yelling at the servants to come with them.

Most all of the hiding servants come out with trepidation and fear, leaving only one woman who is actively fighting back against the men trying to pull her out of the corner. As the rest of them are escorted out of the kitchen area, Creighton walks over to the little hiding place. Two of Creighton's men have this woman by one arm each, but she is struggling against them with all her strength. Creighton touches them both in the shoulder and says "Release her." They both let go of the woman's arms at the same time, and she flops back onto the ground, crawling back against the wall. She appears to be nearly in tears.

Creighton waves the two men off, and they both leave. He then looks down at the woman, and puts out his hand, "We are not here to hurt you. I, am not here to hurt you. All I wish to do is escort you out of this place, away from the blood." The woman looks at his hand, then at his face. After a moment, she reaches out and accepts his hand. Creighton pulls her to her feet, and places his other hand on her back, "Come, let us leave this place. Try not to look at the floor, it will only upset you."

As he escorts the woman out of the kitchen, he notices her taking glances down at the bodies and blood that are strewn across the floor. Neither of them speak a word until they get outside the front gates. The woman gasps, and Creighton's eyes widen. There, in front of the castle, stands Samuel Stoen. To his side is the body of King Drow, and at his feet, is the head. *"I suppose it is King Stoen now…"* Creighton thinks. In front of Stoen and the late-king Drow, the Great Auxiliary, Mallnue Youngstead, is on his knees, held there by Yesha Monroe and two other men. Joppa is there as well, as Stoen is addressing Mallnue, his sword resting on the man's shoulder.

Creighton puts himself in front of the woman, "You do not need to see any more death. Take me to where you live." She looks up at Creighton, then nods, and points to the South, away from where Stoen is conducting his business.

The two of them arrive at where she was leading. It is a large servants quarters building a short walk away from the castle, where the "lesser staff" of the castle would stay, such as cooks like the woman. Despite this, the entire place was empty, except for the woman and Creighton. The rest of the staff who had been escorted out of the castle are being held, it seems. Creighton gestures the woman inside, and closes the door behind them. She walks over to one of the beds and leans her hands on the baseboard. Creighton takes a seat, as she takes a few deep breaths, before saying her first words, "So, do you intend to rape me?"

Creighton shakes his head, "No. I do not partake in such savagery, despite the impression that the events of today may make you think." The woman's body visibly loosens up, and Creighton sees her wipe her sleeve across her eyes. "Alright. Then, why are we here? What do you want?" "I simply wanted to escort you away from the castle, as I was instructed." He responds. "Why not herd me with the rest?" "You seemed more distressed than the others. I wanted to ensure that you were safe."

 She walks over and sits on the edge of one of the beds, "Why are you here? What is all this about?" she asks. Creighton stands up, and walks over to the woman. She is visibly uncomfortable, but does not stand or move from where she is sitting. Joppa's tact is on Creighton's mind. "You, have my most sincere condolences, about all of this, miss. However, this is how change is made." Creighton kneels down in front of her, "Once Stoen is in place, then the blood will end, and the land will be better than it was before. He is a smart man, and has his eyes beyond just the walls of Lockhart. His goal is to make us a stronger, more prosperous territory, which could not happen while Drow still abode in the castle. This all has just been an unfortunate, but necessary, series of events, to accomplish the penultimate goal; prosperity and growth."

The woman sits in silence for a moment, then takes a deep breath. "It sounds like you truly believe in that man…" Creighton nods, the woman sits there in silence, a sorrowful and contemplative look on her face. Creighton reaches up and puts his hand on her shoulder, "My name is Creighton, Creighton Vordana. What may I call you?" She does not respond for a moment, then "Tanta. My name is Tanta."

Chapter #21

Creighton steps back, his sword clasped firmly in both hands. He is facing off against a man in a full bucket style helmet. His opponent lunges in for a strike, but Creighton parries it, slapping his blade to the side. Creighton goes for a short jab to the opponent's stomach, however he takes a step back to avoid it. Creighton quickly pulls his sword back in with a twirl and brings it down in an overhead chop at the shoulder of his opponent, which is avoided with a side-step. Swiftly, the man swings his sword with one hand, and catches Creighton directly in the right cheek.

Creighton stumbles back, almost dropping his sword. He reaches up and touches his cheek, his fingers coming back with red prints. "You, struck my face." Suddenly, his opponent pulls off his helmet, revealing it to be Gesa "Oh! I am sorry Sir Vordana! I did not intend to swing that hard..." Creighton wipes his fingers off on his chest, and walks up to Gesa with a smile, "After all this time, all the practice, you finally land a clean strike!" He says jovially and he slaps Gesa on the shoulder, "Good work, my boy. Just next time, keep in mind we are not actually trying to kill one another." Gesa breathes a sigh of relief, "Yes, sir. Sorry about that."

"No need to apologize. We all can get excited when we have a sword in our hand. This is why we train with blunts, anyhow. I am proud that you have kept to your training."

Lum walks over and gives Gesa a crushing hug from behind, "And I am proud as well! He has gained some sword arms." she says, taking one hand and squeezing his bicep. "Yes, I suppose I have." Gesa replies with a small, proud smile. Tanta walks over and hands Creighton a clean rag for his cheek. The two women had been watching their men spar the whole time. This was the first time that Gesa had ever landed a clean blow on Creighton.

Creighton balls up the rag and presses it into his cheek. The wound is nothing major, barely deeper than a paper cut. Besides, the cut did not outweigh the pride he felt in Gesa. It has not been an easy road, a lot of bruises and being knocked down for the boy. The greatest goal for any mentor is to be surpassed by their pupil, and while he may not quite be there yet, Creighton sees great promise in Gesa.

As he is pressing his wound, he sees Lia Benton walking down the road leading a pair of cows, Hatch in front of him carrying a huge sack of corn, telling one of his many stories loudly for all to hear. Lia makes eye contact with Creighton, sneers, and nods his head at Hatch. Creighton just shrugs, Lia rolls his eyes in annoyance and looks straight-ahead again. Tanta grabs Creighton's arm and snuggles with it, "You have done such a great job with his training." "He was a good student." Creighton replies.

Lum whispers something into Gesa's ear, and Gesa looks at Creighton "Sorry, sir, but I need to go. Do I have your permission?" Creighton nods, Gesa and Lum walk away together. Creighton looks around, "Where is my son?" Tanta looks behind her, where Creighton II was sitting. "He was watching on the bench. Hmm..." Creighton walks over to the backside of his home and leans his sword against the rear wall, then he and Tanta walk around the front of their home.

Creighton looks through the front window and does not see his son inside. Tanta calls out for him, but does not get a response. "I am sure he is in town somewhere. You look south, I will go north." Tanta nods and begins walking toward the south of the town. Neither of them are particularly scared or worried, Creighton II never goes too far from home. Creighton walks down the main road of the town, looking back and forth for any sign of his boy.

"He may be with Forda" Creighton thinks, still holding the bloody rag to his cheek. Forda is one of Creighton II's friends, a boy the same age, around 4-5 years, but Creighton II is about a head taller and quite heavier than him. Creighton walks over to Forda's home and knocks on the door, after a moment Forda's father answers. "Oh, um, how can I help you, Vordana?" he asks. "Is my boy here with yours?" The father shakes his head, "No. Your son has not come over in a few days." Creighton nods in response, then turns around and walks away.

Creighton stands in the middle of the street, crosses his arms, and thinks… then it occurs to him. *"I think that my wood cutting ax was not where I left it"*. Creighton walks back in the direction of his house, then turns off the street toward the woodline. Creighton touches his cheek with his fingers, and feels that the blood has stopped coming, he tosses the blood-soaked rag to the side. Very shortly after entering the woods, he hears the exact sound that he expected; the whacking of wood.

The previous week, Creighton had taken his son out and showed him how to chop logs, cut branches, and so on. He knew that the boy was not physically capable of cleaving through a proper log, but it was a good lesson to teach young. He looks back and forth, then spots him. His son holding his wood cutting ax, swinging away at a fully grown tree. While it is nowhere near coming down, the boy has made a surprising amount of progress. Also all around him are sticks, branches and chunks of bark that have been cleaved into multiple pieces.

"Creighton, my son!" Creighton calls out. Creighton II stops cutting and turns around to face his father, "Hi father!" he says with a big, tired smile on his face. "Why are you out here by yourself?" The boy grips the ax in both hands, "Well, you and mama were busy. So I wanted to cut down a tree for us." Creighton chuckles, "And why do we need a full tree?" The son shrugs, "Fire?" Creighton walks over and puts his hand on his son's shoulder, "We cannot burn a fresh tree like this, my son. It has to be dead, and dried out. If you were to cut this down, and we were to piece it apart, we would not be able to use it for three seasons."

Creighton takes the ax from his son, "In addition, you never cut down a tree alone. Always have another person with you. To share the work, and also be able to help you in case something happens. A tree like this one, would crush you dead if it fell on you, or at the least break any bones that were trapped under it. Also the worry of animals. Do you understand?" Creighton II nods his head, "Yes. Sorry, father." Creighton claps his shoulder, "No need for apologies, my boy. Just learn from my words, and do not run off into the woods alone."

Creighton steps to his son's side, and pushes him forward, "Now, come with me. Your mother is concerned for you." The two of them begin walking back out of the woods, Creighton looks around. It looked like an angry beaver had a fit of anger in this little section of the woods. Some of the things that young Creighton II chopped and cut were fairly thick, things that Creighton himself would have had to take a couple swings at to get through. Did the boy get through all of them with one swing? Likely not, but it was still impressive nonetheless.

Creighton and Creighton II make it back to their home, where Tanta is sitting outside. She sees the two of them coming and waves, "There you are. Where was he, my love?" Creighton pats his son on the back, "He was out in the woods, trying to cut us down a tree. Unfortunately, he was not able to down it on his own." Tanta smiles, "Maybe some day, you will be able to cut this whole forest down on your own." Creighton II smiles, excited at the thought.

"Vordana's!" the gruff voice of Hatch Delgoss rings out from down the street, "Come down to my home!" After he says that, he turns and runs back toward his own house. Tanta stands and grabs Creighton II's hand, "What could be the matter?" She asks out loud, "I do not know, but we should go." All three of them begin walking down toward the Delgoss home.

Once they arrive, they open the front door and walk in. Inside is the entire Delgoss family, Gesa Het's parents, Gesa, and Lia Benton. Everyone except for Lia is in the common area around the table, Lia is in his sleeping quarters with a bottle of liquor, reading a book. As the Vordana family enter, Hatch claps his hands, "Everyone is here! Now, Gesa, Lum. What is this all about?"

Gesa and Lum both get up from their seats and walk over to the head of the table. The two of them put their arms around each other, and Lum is the one to speak up. "Thank you for coming, those of you who do not live in this home. As you all know, Gesa and I have been *seeing each other* for quite some time now, and we have only grown more fond of one another's company. We spoke this morning, and a decision was made...” “We are going to wed!” Gesa says loudly and proudly. Everyone in the room smiles and claps, Hatch walks over and grips both of them in a big hug, while Gesa's parents sit quietly and smile. Creighton is filled with pride, and Tanta clutches his arm, her heart feeling warm. Creighton notices Unet brushing away some tears.

Once Hatch releases them, Lum gets her breath back, “Once we have the ceremony, we will be taking ourselves to live in Hikline. Gesa has an uncle who will gladly house us for some time, and I have always wanted to try my hand at the Lea.” Gesa speaks next, “And, I want to thank all of you for all you have done for me. The Delgoss family for welcoming me into their family, my parents obviously, and Sir Creighton Vordana, for helping teach me the way of the sword, and helping me grow into a man.” Creighton walks over and places his hand on Gesa's shoulder, “It was my pleasure to be your teacher, Gesa.” He looks at Lum, “You are quite lucky.”

Gesa looks up at Creighton, then throws his arms around him, giving a hug to Creighton, who does not quite know how to react. “Um, thank you...” Gesa lets go, then turns back to Lum, and the two embrace in a kiss. Kentra, sitting at the table, upends her glass that was assuredly filled with strong drink, emptying it quickly into her belly.

Chapter #22

The day is very sunny and warm, Creighton and Tanta Vordana are outside of their home, Creighton leaning on the wall and Tanta sitting in the dirt, both watching their son at play with the other boys of the village. A smile is stuck to Tanta's face, "He is so big" she says with pride Creighton nods in agreement, crossing his arms, "He will be a very large man, I am sure." At just over six years, his head already reaches to the chest of his mother. Tanta leans her head on Creighton's leg, "It seems it was just last night that I fed him from my body." Creighton kneels down to be closer to his wife, "You clearly fed him well."

Creighton II is tussling with two of the other young boys, one of them being his friend Forda. Forda jumps onto Creighton II's back, wrapping his arms around his neck. Despite them being only a few months apart, Creighton is significantly larger than Forda. Creighton II grabs the boy's arms from around his neck and tosses him a short distance to his right. Forda hits the ground hard, knocking him a little dizzy. The other boy, the son of the local farmer that is two years older than Creighton II, grabs him around the waste and picks him up, with some struggle.

Creighton II is quickly able to escape from the boy's shoulder. He lands on his feet behind the boy and grabs him around the stomach. Creighton II begins to squeeze the boy's belly, he tries to pry Creighton's hands apart but can not. After a moment of squeezing, Creighton lifts the older boy into the air, taking his feet a short distance from the ground. "I give, I give..." The older boy says with a shortness of breath. Creighton II lets the older boy down, who immediately begins to pant, trying to get his breath back.

Creighton begins to clap his hands loudly, "Good fighting my son!" Creighton II looks over to his parents with a smile. Forda's mother walks over to her son to check on him. The older boy finishes catching his breath, then charges full-force at Creighton II again. "Should we tell him to be more gentle, my love?" Tanta asks Creighton, "Nonsense." he responds, "We do not want him to think his strength is a bad thing, it will serve him well as a man. Besides, being that young, it is impossible to be truly hurt" Tanta nods, "You are right. I am just afraid he will harm the others." Creighton nods his head "If he hurts a boy, his mother will care for him, and he will grow tougher for it." Tanta stands up, "I suppose so."

Creighton calls out to his son, "Creighton, bid the other boys farewell! Get inside and pull on your boots. We must go hunt!" Creighton II picks up the older boy and tosses him aside, then looks back at his father and nods in acknowledgement, before running inside their home, Creighton and Tanta watch him go. Creighton looks back at the boy that was tossed aside, "He will one day be a much sought-over warrior."

Creighton and Tanta go inside, he sits down at their table with a drink as Creighton II dresses himself for the hunt. "We are going to do some stationary hunting tonight, my son. Get where we wish to sit now, and let the prey come to us." A Creighton also begins to change, he finds himself thinking of Gesa, and the last time the two of them hunted. *"I hope he and Lum are enjoying Hikline."* Creighton had recommended that they talk to Renda, and tell her that he sent them. She would be able to help them get settled in town. Tanta walks over and picks up one of her gowns, laying it on the table. Tanta finds the small tear in her skirt and pinches the sides in her fingers, "This is one of my favorite pieces, I hope that this will keep it from tearing more." She begins to stitch, Creighton finishes dressing for the hunt, while his son is still pulling on his shoes.

Creighton hears the sound of a howling wolf. He looks out the window, "It seems early in the day for dogs to be up and about" Creighton thinks to himself, giving it little concern. Then, there is the sound of another, and another, and barking. Creighton quickly walks over to the cabinet where he keeps all of his weapons and gear, and pulls out his prime sword. Tanta looks up at him, "Is something concerning you?" Then she hears it as well, "Wolves?" Creighton nods his head, "It sounds like..." The sound of a screaming child fills the air. *"It is happening…"* Tanta stands as quickly as to knock her chair to the floor, Creighton pulls a shortsword from the cabinet and hands it to her. "Lock the door, keep the boy safe."

Outside is the sound of commotion and screaming, and wolves are charging in from the woods. Without seeing, Creighton would guess more than the average pack. Twenty, thirty, maybe more. Creighton comes out, sword pulled and ready, and it was worse than he could have imagined. There are wolves everywhere, he cannot even begin to count. Creighton looks left and right, there is a wolf at every door. Creighton hears something behind him, he turns to be met with a wolf. It lunges at Creighton, but he avoids its bite, and quickly skewers it through the neck.

As Creighton pulls his sword free, he sees Hatch come out of his home with his own sword. "Where is Lia?!" Creighton calls out, "Should be with the cows!" Hatch responds, as a wolf sprints at him from between two houses. However, Hatch is able to kick it in the face, before driving his sword through the animal's chest. "Have you seen Kentra?!" Hatch calls out to Creighton, responds "I have not!" before running toward where Hatch keeps his cattle. Keeping his vigilance, the sounds of wolves and human anguish are all around him.

He wants to help, but he cannot help everyone, and he needs the assistance of Lia. Creighton makes it to where the cattle are being kept, all the cattle are panicking, in great fear. He calls out "Lia?!" to no response. Creighton runs into the barn, where he sees a dead body. He jogs over to the body and rolls it over, it is not Lia. Just another man from town, with his throat completely open. Suddenly Creighton is tackled by a wolf, knocked onto his back, managing to keep hold of his sword. The wolf goes to bite him, but Creighton feeds the animal his jacketed forearm. Creighton swings his sword up into the neck of the wolf, causing it to yelp and let go, the blade digging into its fur. He grabs the wolf by the throat and plunges his sword upward into its jaw, and through the top of its head.

He pushes the animal off of him, stands up, and calls out again "LIA?!" Once again, no response. "Damn it, where is that bastard?!" Creighton says to himself, as he runs out of the barn. *If I cannot find Lia, I need to get home"* he thinks as he runs. In that short time that he was at the barn, there are more bodies in the street, and more screams coming from homes. Creighton steps over a few bloodied corpses, and he hears a familiar voice screaming, "HELP! HELP!" over near the community woodshed, Kentra on her back, a wolf on top of her biting her hand, and another biting her leg.

Breaking into a sprint, Creighton makes his way down the street. As he is running, a man bursts out of his front window with a wolf biting the back of his neck, *"Cannot save everyone"* he thinks sorrowfully as he continues to run toward Kentra. Creighton gets to Kentra, and punts the wolf that is latched onto her hand, knocking it off of her. He takes his sword and swings it upwards at the one biting Kentra's leg, slashing its throat. The one he kicked has stood back up, Creighton thrusts his sword out and catches it in the eye, killing it instantly.

Creighton looks down at Kentra, and kneels down. She is missing two fingers, her leg is bleeding profusely, and she has several other bites. She is in really bad shape... Kentra is hyperventilating. "Can you walk?" Kentra shakes her head. Creighton looks over at the community wood shed, and gets an idea. He runs over and opens the doors, then back over to Kentra, "Come, you can hide in here." Creighton sets his sword down and grabs Kentra up under both of her arms. He drags Kentra, who tries to help with her non-bitten leg. Creighton props her against the wall of the shed, she barely has enough room to fit, "I will come and get you once all this is done." She looks up at him, and nods. "Thank you."

He closes the doors to the shed and latches them, then goes and picks his sword back up. In the distance he hears the sounds of shattering glass, and a scream, Tanta's scream. Creighton's adrenaline dumps and he sprints back toward his home. He makes it there in only seconds, slamming himself against his front door, knowing it was locked, and smashing it off the hinges. Tanta is kneeling on the floor, clutching her son, and there is a dead wolf on the floor, sword still stuck in its throat. Creighton walks over and kneels in front of them, "Tanta". She looks up, tears in her eyes, and a giant bite mark across her face.

Creighton is filled with sorrow, anger, and fear all at once. He reaches over and pulls the sword from the throat of the wolf, "Take this. Take this and you need to go. Now." Tanta looks behind Creighton and points, "Behind you." Creighton stands and spins around, sword readied. He expects to see a wolf, but instead, he sees a man. A man covered from heel to hair, his face and head wrapped thoroughly to cover his identity. In his hands are two swords, both identical to each other, and both with fresh blood on them.

"Who are you?!" Creighton calls out, stepping toward the man. He stays silent for a moment, then "I... am King Drow's vengeance." With that, Creighton lunges at the man with two swords, swinging at his head, but the strike is blocked. Creighton advances on the man, and the man walks backward out of the doorway. Creighton swings again, but his sword is slapped aside. The man with two swords attempts a stab to the stomach, but Creighton dodges. Creighton kicks the man in the abdomen, knocking him backwards.

Tanta runs out of their home, Creighton II's hand in one hand and a sword in her other. Creighton looks at her and screams "Take the boy and run! Now!" She turns and sprints toward the woods. The man with two swords slashes at Creighton, who is almost able to avoid but gets a small cut across his chest. The blade glanced him, but still went through his jacket and broke the skin... Creighton steps back and returns with a thrust, which is slapped down and the man goes for a slash at Creighton's throat, which misses.

Creighton grips his sword with both hands, turns the blade, and pulls it to the side, slashing the man's left leg. He winces and takes a step back, unfortunately the cut was not very deep, due to the lack of velocity, but it still drew blood. Before Creighton can follow through, he is hit with a wolf from his side. It grabs on to his right arm, pulling it down. Creight knees the animal in the throat, and throws it off, then stomps with all his weight on its neck.

The man with two swords lunges at Creighton, sticking him in the right side, causing Creighton to yell in pain, before swinging his fist and almost catching the man in the head. He pulls both his swords back and tries to slash at Creighton's throat and his stomach again. The throat slash misses, but the cut to the stomach makes its mark, but not as deep as the man likely wanted. Creighton swings his sword wildly in his right hand only, missing as the man ducked, however this gives him the chance to grip his sword in both hands, and come back with a swing to the man's side, which connects full-force.

The power of the strike knocks the man stumbling to the ground. Creighton looks down at him, no blood... the outside of his clothing is leather, which the blade cut through, but under that is steel plate. Creighton lifts his sword to take the man's head off, when his leg is grabbed from behind by another wolf. Creighton tries to kick it off, when another wolf charges him, but Creighton is able to take that one out with a slash of his sword. He is able to get the beast off his leg, and take its head off with one, contempt-filled chop.

The man with the two swords has gotten back to his feet and charges. He unleashes a flurry of slashes and strikes at Creighton, who manages to block most of them, except a moderate blow to the left bicep, which drew some blood. Creighton manages to parry one strike, and go for a shoulder blow, which the man back steps away from. Crieghton goes for a lunge at the face, but the man ducks and strikes the sword upwards. Creighton almost loses his grip, as the man slashes his left thigh.

Creighton grunts in pain, then with all his might, push-kicks the man in his chest. This sends the man sprawling back, but his footing is quickly regained. "Come on you bastard, this cannot be all you have in you!" calls out Creighton in anger. Suddenly, a sharp, intense pain shoots up his back. "*I... cannot feel my legs...*" He loses almost all feeling below his waist, his arms begin to tingle, and he falls to his knees.

His body lurches, as whatever struck him is wrenched from his back. From behind Creighton, comes Lia Benton, his hatchet covered in fresh, dripping blood. Lia looks at his fellow general, "It does not make me happy to do this, General Vordana. It is just the way things have gone." Lia looks back to the man with two swords, "The Delgoss man and his wife are dead, along with everyone else on that end of town."

Lia wipes the blood from his hatchet on his pants, "I will continue to make sure that everyone else meets the same fate, sir." With that, Lia walks away, Creighton watching him go. The man with two swords walks up to Creighton, and places one blade on each side of his neck. "For King Drow." As Creighton looks up, he sees something hanging out of the man's face coverings. A few strands, of blue hair... Creighton's final thoughts, as his head falls from his shoulders, are of Tanta and his son...

Epilogue

The sun is bright and the wind is low, as Brandon Boldwood stands out back of his smithy, trying to find good wood for sword grips, it is a warm day as the sun is glistening off of his shaved bald head, and his sideburns are dripping. He and his assistant, a man named Felc, received an order for ten shortswords, a simple order, but they were fresh out of pre-made grips. He lives in an average sized town, about a hundred and fifty people within it, called Arling, and he runs the local smithing shop, or 'smithy.' Brandon takes the utmost pride in his work, so no splintered, swollen log will do. Most of the trees in and around his town are pine, which while not Brandon's preferred wood, it served well enough. Soft, but it can be treated to be stiff enough to serve his purposes.

Normally he would make a request of oak or birch, but the order needs to be fulfilled before the next group of traders come through the town. As Brandon is looking for a suitable piece of wood, his assistant, Felc, pokes his head out of the rear window of the shop, "Master Boldwood, we are nearly out of water inside." Boldwood does not look up from the wood, "Alright. What are you doing currently?" "I am cutting and shaping leather for the sheaths, master." Brandon sighs, that is an important task, "Well keep doing that I suppose. I will go fetch us some more. Place our vases out front for me, quickly."

Felc pulls his head back inside, and Brandon grabs a small cart that they keep around the back for dragging various things around. He pulls it behind him to the front of the smithy, where Felc is pulling around the last of their three vases that they use to store drinking and cooking water. Like many other towns, the majority of their water comes from the clean river a short walk from the town-proper. Brandon loads the vases onto the cart, grabs their filling jug, and pushes the cart down the street, toward the pathway to the river.

Brandon rolls his neck, thinking about the order. He and his assistant should be able to accomplish this in the next two or three days, as long as there are no delays. Brandon keeps a small selection of weaponry and tools on-hand at all times, of course, but the customer was very adamant that they wanted them all new and identical, which Brandon is happy to do. He loves making new things, and the desired cut and shape of these swords are something that Brandon has never done before.

For whatever reason, they want the tips of the swords rounded, like a disc, and sharpened all the way around. A strange design, Brandon thinks. Not really good for stabbing, or for slashing, in his experienced opinion. But it is what the man asked for, and it will be a new experience for Brandon and Felc. *"Maybe they are for ceremonies, or games"* Brandon thinks. He has never encountered such a blade on the battlefield, where he spent most of his young years, and he encountered many strange things in his time. Some were more innovative or intelligent than others.

That was part of what inspired Brandon to take up smithing, once he decided that warrior life had outlived its interest for him. The mechanics of weaponry, how and why it all works, what goes into making it. Back when he was still on the battlefield, he had never operated a forge or filed a blade before. But the job had always been of interest to him. As a man of the blade, how could it not have been? Although his preferred weapon was never a sword or a spear, he liked the power and the feeling of a good ax, when he was in conflict.

Brandon makes it down to the bank of the river, and pushes his cart over near the mouth of the river, as it is easier and cleaner to fill directly from there. Brandon takes the filling jug and puts it below the water, and as he is observing the area around him, he sees something he is shocked that he missed... across from him on the other bank, there is a boy laying unmoving, and what looks to be a wolf laying next to him.

Brandon quickly drops the filling jug to the dirt and runs a short way down the bank, to where he knows it is most shallow, and runs across the narrow river. Once he makes it to the other side, he jogs over to where the two are laying. First, Brandon looks at the wolf, who is motionless, its jaw snapped to the side and its fur matted down from the water. Confident that the wolf is dead, Brandon kneels down next to the child. A very large boy, with long black hair and tan skin, lying on his back. Brandon reaches down and places his hand around the boy's neck, feeling for a heartbeat.

The boy's eyes open slowly, and he looks up at Brandon, who immediately takes his hand from around the boy's neck. The boy reaches up toward him, weakly, Brandon grabs his hand "Yes, hello. Can you speak? Is anything broken?" Brandon looks back at the wolf, "Did that attack you?" The boy utters, "Mom...", before his eyes close again, and his arm droops. Brandon quickly pulls the boy up into his arms, and runs back the path he came from, leaving his cart.

Brandon starts running down the trail back to town, not knowing how close to death this boy is. After a run that took less than half the time of his trek out there, he makes it back to his shop and calls out "Felc!" as he kicks the door to his shop open. His assistant, Felc, runs over, "What is it master? Oh, who is that?" He asks, as he notices what Brandon is carrying. "I do not know, he was by the river. Go fetch Tynion, now!" Without response, Felc runs out of the smithy, to go find the man that Brandon demanded.

Brandon looks around his cluttered and messy workshop, then eyes a bench covered in leather scraps and ties. He reaches up with his boot and clears off all the things with one sweep of his foot, then lays the boy down on the bench. Brandon looks around the room, "Fire is already going... he needs a blanket, or something..." Brandon says, thinking out loud to himself. As Brandon is running around looking for something to cover the boy, he sits up straight, and starts coughing.

Brandon returns to him and kneels down, "There, there, boy. Cough as much as you need. Are you cold? Does anything hurt?" The boy takes a deep breath and shakes his head, "N... no. I, I think I am alright. Nothing hurts strongly." Brandon nods, "Good, that is good. I am Brandon Boldwood, and I found you over near the river. What is your name? And what happened to you? Did that wolf attack you while you were at play?" The boy takes some deep breaths, then replies, "My name is Creighton, Vordana. Named for my father. And, the wolf..." he pauses, Brandon is struck with familiarity. Why does he know that name...? Then he realizes.

"Vordana. Is your father a large man, fairly tall, wide jaw, blond hair?" The boy nods, "Yes." Brandon stands, one of his fellow generals when he was in Stoen's Legion, that was why he knew the name. "Interesting. Where is he now? Does he live near?" The boy does not speak, then begins to shake, "Are you alright?" Brandon asks, placing his hand on the boy's shoulder. "The... there was a man. And wolves. There were wolves, in the town, and... my father was fighting them. My mother took me to the river, threw me into the water. But, she..."

"Wolves?" Brandon thinks, but suddenly his mind is struck with a letter that he received several years ago. Packs of wolves attacking towns, towns with generals from Stoen's Legion, and the fates of the generals. Brandon clasps both of his hands behind his head, this was not good. There has not been a reported survivor of one of these attacks before, and this one, is the son of one of the generals. Would the man taking these wolves around come for him?

Brandon strokes his jaw, then kneels down next to the boy, and places his hand on his shoulder. "Listen, I need you to pay attention to my words. Understand?" Creighton looks at Brandon, then looks at his feet, and nods. Brandon takes a deep breath, "This may be confusing for you, but I need you to trust me. I am sad for what happened to your parents, and I am sad for what happened to your town. However, I have a fear that what happened there, may also happen here."

The boy's eyes get really wide with fear, "That is why you must listen to me. Your name, Creighton Vordana, yes?" Creighton nods. "Listen to me, very carefully. That is no longer your name, at least for the time-being. That name, your fathers name, it may put you in danger. It may bring the ire of the man who attacked your town, and brought the wolves. Do you understand?" The boy looks at his feet, then back to Brandon, "Y-yes, yes I understand." Brandon nods, "Good, that is good. You are not to say that that is your name, you are not to answer when called by it. Do you understand me with complete clarity?"

The boy nods, Brandon stands up. "Excellent. Our town healer will be here shortly, and he will check on you, make sure you are not more wounded than you feel." Brandon grabs a stool and pulls it over to the boy's side, "After that, you can stay with me for now. Do you have any extended family near? An aunt, a grandparent?" Creighton shakes his head, "No, I have none." Brandon nods, "Alright, then I shall care for you for now. Is that agreeable?" The boy swallows, and nods. His shaking has subsided as he looks around the smithy, "Is, is this your home?" Brandon chuckles, "No, this is my workshop. My true home is near, but not nearly this dirty."

In walks Tynion Luv, the town healer, with Felc shortly behind him, "Where is the child?" he asks, with a calm and gentle tone. Brandon waves him over, "Right here." He stands up, offering his stool to Tynion, who walks over and sets his small bag of supplies down. "What is your name, child?" Tynion asks, as he sits down by his side. The boy opens his mouth, then looks up at Brandon, who crosses his arms. "His name is Krandos. Krandos Aleauntos."

Epilogue II

Samuel Stoen is walking down the hall of his castle, daoned in his armor as he usually is, toward his planning room. He has received word that there has been another wolf attack, he walks into the room, "Where was it this time?!" he calls out to the staff who were already in there. "King Stoen, it was in a small town by the river, Stonewater." The king taps his chin, "Stonewater... who was in Stonewater?"

"Creighton Vordana, sir!" Calls out a voice from behind. "Joppa Jak used to live there as well, however he was reported to have moved to the north quite some time ago." It is the voice of Mallnue Youngstead. King Stoen slaps his thigh, "There is my Great Auxiliary. It was good of you to come so quickly." Mallnue nods, "I was down in the library, doing some research. I came as soon as I heard my name was being called." He walks in, favoring his right leg.

"Why the limp?" Stoen asks. "Oh, that? I was reading a book and pacing, and accidentally kicked a table. That is all." King Stoen laughs, "A silly injury, Mallnue. Now come, we must discuss what has happened." "Yes sir, I shall read the report for the room." Mallnue says, as he picks up the paper, and brushes his long blue bangs out from in front of his face.

Thank you to everyone who took the time to read this book,
my first ever dive into the world of published writing.
I hope you enjoyed the time spent.

A special thank you to my Dad, Jarrad, & Sande for
reviewing this book and giving me their feedback.

Please look for book 2 of the series,
Inferni Ensium: Tempering,
coming soon.

Once again, please head over to PurifiedMadness.com for
more information on the Inferni Ensium series, or check out
Purified Madness on social media.

Copyright © 2021 Z.J. Markel

Unfamiliar Words & Phrases

Territory
* A large portion of land separated by theoretical borders and governed by a centralized ruler, like a state or a country.

Sword Arms
* A specific and identifiable way that a person's arms grow due to sword / weapons training.

Shield Carrier
* Soldier whose entire job on the battlefield is to carry around a large shield to provide cover for others. Generally a new recruit.

Prime Sword / Weapon
* A person's primary weapon of choice, that they are most trained with.

Charge Soldier
* Soldiers who are on the front lines, charging into battle ahead of all others.

Tat Bull
* A heavily built wild ox with backswept horns, infamous for being hard to domesticate and very dumb.

Helda
* Alcohol with basil leaves in it, used to clean wounds.

Warrior Surge
* Soldier whose entire job on the battlefield is to carry around a large shield to provide cover for others. Generally a recruit.

Great Auxiliary
  • The King/High Prominence Ruler's second-in-command and advisor.

Wagon Merchant
  • A traveling salesman who sells wares out of a wagon.

Cattle-Master
  • Someone who is trained and experienced in dealing with cattle, oftentimes found operating bull-pulled wagons.

Dirt Rat
  • Rodent with a heavy body and short legs.

Lea
  • An arena where live combat is held, usually for entertainment purposes.

Table of Contents